MISSING PERSONS
The First Buddy Steel Mystery

"*Missing Persons* is a cracking series debut and Buddy Steel is a protagonist bound to have a long shelf life."

—Reed Farrel Coleman, *New York Times* bestselling author
of *What You Break*

"Fans of Parker's work will appreciate Buddy, another irreverent, complex lawman."

—*Library Journal*

"Michael Brandman's follow-up to the three Jesse Stone novels he adeptly penned for the late Robert B. Parker gives us the cool and iconic Buddy Steel. A former point guard turned cop, Steel damn sure owns the ground he walks on. All capable 6'3" and one-hundred-seventy pounds of him, Buddy's that guy that you want to ride with when s..t hits the fan. With plenty of thrilling moments and turns you don't see coming, what a great ride Brandman takes us on in *Missing Persons*. Trust me, you won't be disappointed. Buckle up."

—Robert Knott, *New York Times* bestselling author of
the Hitch and Cole Series

One on One

Books by Michael Brandman

The Jesse Stone Novels
Robert B. Parker's Killing the Blues
Robert B. Parker's Fool Me Twice
Robert B. Parker's Damned If You Do

The Buddy Steel Mysteries
Missing Persons
One on One

One on One

A Buddy Steel Mystery

Michael Brandman

Poisoned Pen Press

First Edition 2018

10 9 8 7 6 5 4 3 2 1

Library of Congress Control Number: 2018933529

ISBN: 9781464210273   Hardcover
ISBN: 9781464210297   Trade Paperback
ISBN: 9781464210303   Ebook

Poisoned Pen Press
4014 N. Goldwater Blvd., #201
Scottsdale, AZ 85251
www.poisonedpenpress.com
info@poisonedpenpress.com

Printed in the United States of America

As always...

...for Joanna...

...my shining star.

"Maybe all one can do is
hope to end up with
the right regrets."

—*Arthur Miller*

Chapter One

The late summer sun was making its steady ascent into a cloudless morning sky when my cell phone rang.

I broke stride, mopping the sweat from my forehead with my t-shirt. Still fighting for breath, I grabbed the phone from the pocket of my running shorts, and flipped it open. "Buddy Steel."

I had been jogging along a barren stretch of Freedom Beach, all the while sidestepping mounds of dried and drying seaweed that disfigured the grainy white sand. A pair of gulls eyed me suspiciously. The smell of burnt wood rose from the remains of a beach fire.

"Sorry, Buddy," Sheriff's Deputy Johnny Kennerly's disembodied voice crackled into the phone. "But we've got one."

"One what?"

"One that requires your presence."

"Perhaps you might want to be a little less obtuse, John."

"Henry Carson."

"Who's Henry Carson?"

"Assistant Principal."

"Where?"

"Freedom High."

"What about him?"

"Well, for one thing, he's dead."

"And for another?"

"It appears he was murdered."

● ● ● ● ●

Still in my running shorts, but having added a green Boston Celtic hoodie, I pulled my Sheriff's cruiser to a stop in front of Freedom High School.

A phalanx of news personnel and their equipment, along with a handful of gawkers, had already gathered and several began shouting questions at me as I strode past them and into the building. I was met at the door by Sheriff's Deputy Marsha Russo.

"Nice legs," she commented as I approached her.

"Witty. Where's Carson?"

"In his office. Fourth floor."

We stepped into the closest elevator and Marsha pressed four.

"Talk to me," I said.

"Not pretty. Killer used a steak knife."

At the fourth floor, the doors opened onto a chaotic scene. The narrow hallway was filled with small groupings of students, most of them simply standing around watching the goings on in silence. One young woman was crying.

"What are they doing here?"

"Classes have been suspended for the day."

"Can we disperse them? Get them out of here."

"Be my pleasure," Marsha said as she led me to Henry Carson's office, a small room, sparsely furnished, with a single window that overlooked an air shaft.

Johnny Kennerly stood in front of the office door, in conversation with Coroner Norma Richard. A team of State forensic officers huddled together, awaiting the green-light to begin their investigation.

I nodded to each of them, then followed Johnny into Henry Carson's office.

"You're the first one in," Kennerly said.

"After how many school personnel?"

"The building maintenance supervisor. The principal. A security officer. No one else."

"They disturb anything?"

"Not that any of them will admit. Maintenance man found him when he was making his morning rounds."

I stepped carefully around several pools of blood and approached the body. The late Mr. Carson was seated on a wooden armchair in front of his desk, facedown, a stainless-steel steak knife protruding from his neck.

Large quantities of blood had flooded the desk en route to the unpolished wood floor where it had congealed.

I stepped away and looked around the office, a cramped affair boasting a desk, the armchair on which the body now rested, a pair of straight-backed chairs facing the desk, and two wall-sized bookcases, each filled to overflowing.

I turned to Johnny. "What do you think?"

"I think he's dead."

"That's very helpful, John."

"Should we admit the hordes?"

"I don't see why not."

I stepped to the door and motioned for Marsha Russo to join us. "You know the drill?"

Marsha nodded.

"Is there a Mrs. Carson?"

"There is," Kennerly said.

"Does she know?"

"Principal phoned her."

"I'll want to talk with her. And the principal. Would you please make appointments for me with both of them? I'm going home to change clothes. I'll be back in an hour."

"You'll inform the Sheriff," John said.

I nodded.

"And Her Honor?"

I nodded again.

"Some fine way to start the week," Marsha said.

I shook my head in agreement. "It's always something."

Chapter Two

The Sheriff to whom John referred is my father, the Honorable Burton Steel, Senior, now in his third term but currently debilitated by the early onset of Amyotrophic Lateral Sclerosis, ALS, otherwise known as Lou Gehrig's disease.

Her Honor is my father's wife, my stepmother, the estimable Regina Goodnow, the Mayor of Freedom. I stopped by their house, my childhood home, to deliver the news in person.

As is generally the case when I get my first glimpse of my father these days, I'm forced to conceal my shock at the level of his deterioration. Once a powerful and towering figure, the old man's disease had diminished him considerably.

When he had received his diagnosis, he summoned me and insisted I join him in the San Remo County Sheriff's Department. I had been living in Los Angeles, an LAPD homicide detective attached to the Hollywood division. Conflicted as I was about him and our at-best testy relationship, I answered his call and returned to Freedom and a lifestyle that grew disagreeable quickly.

My life was further complicated by his continued insistence that I be prepared to assist him in taking his own life whenever he deemed it advisable.

We had a great deal of unfinished business between us,

but the encroaching ethical challenge was paramount in my mind. It took precedence over any presumed detente we might somehow manage to achieve.

When I arrived at the house, he was seated at the breakfast table in his bathrobe and slippers, a plate of uneaten scrambled eggs and sourdough toast growing cold in front of him. He looked up at me and muttered, "Murdered?"

"Murder? Someone was murdered?" my stepmother inquired as she bustled into the kitchen.

As usual, she regarded me warily, at once on her guard and, as always, ready to spring to the offense regarding any issue on which she and I might disagree. Which meant nearly everything.

"Did you offer Buddy some breakfast?" she asked my father, who mumbled some kind of unintelligible response.

She turned to me. "Buddy? Coffee? Eggs? Anything?"

"Thank you, Regina. I'm fine."

"Burton's not eating," she proclaimed, ignoring the fact that my father was still in the room. "The doctor keeps telling him he needs to eat in order to keep up his strength. But does he listen? Not on your life, does he listen. Look at him. He looks anorexic. He refuses to eat."

The Sheriff didn't respond. I could detect the first spark of anger igniting in him.

"What's this about a murder?" the Mayor asked, taking a seat across from my father.

"Henry Carson," I said.

"Who?"

"Freedom High. Assistant principal. Stabbed to death."

"Stabbed," she said. "My God, how gruesome."

"I wanted you both to know." I hoped to appease the two birds with a single stone.

My father gazed at me through sorrowful eyes that begged

compassion for his diminished faculties. His voice, once so forceful and commanding, had been reduced to a scratchy whisper. "Where?"

"In his office."

"Suspects?"

"None yet. But I'm just starting. I'll keep you in the loop."

"Does the press have the story?" Regina quizzed me. "Will I be asked for a comment?"

I inwardly smiled in wonder at how she always managed to make herself the center of any and every event. Her question was a rhetorical one. My guess was she had already determined in which order she would summon her makeup, hair, and sartorial team. Her public relations reps, also. "A murder won't reflect well on Freedom."

"I'm sure you'll charm the press in your usual manner, Regina."

"She's got the fucking media in her back pocket," the Sheriff rasped.

"Oh, Burton," she yammered, "must you always be so profane?"

Which I took as my cue to get out of there.

Chapter Three

"She wouldn't talk with me," Marsha Russo said. "Claims the doctor put her on some kind of sedative that made her gaga. They'd been married for less than a year. All she would say is she can't imagine who would want to kill him. I told her we needed to speak with her."

"And?"

"She hung up."

"Try again later."

Marsha nodded.

We were seated in my office at the Freedom Town Hall where the Sheriff's Department was housed. Marsha had been joined by Johnny Kennerly and Sheriff's Deputy Al Striar. All three were longtime department veterans, appointed by my father in his first term. Each wore a Sheriff's uniform, smartly tailored and pressed.

I, on the other hand, wore my outfit of choice: jeans, an L.L. Bean light-blue work shirt, a brown Ralph Lauren corduroy jacket, and Filson work boots.

I rarely if ever wear a uniform—for reasons stemming back to the days when my old man was a street cop. He had purchased a boy's size police uniform, a junior version of his own, and had decorated it with medals and awards. He frequently forced me to wear it.

He was forever dragging me to all kinds of police-sponsored events where I was shoved forward as a kind of gussied up Mini-Me version of himself, the uniformed scion of a steadfast police officer whose sights were already set on bigger things.

As I grew, my mother repeatedly tailored the uniform until finally there wasn't enough fabric left to take out. The uniform became smaller and fit more tightly. Until the night I grabbed a pair of scissors and decimated the fucking thing. Which was the official end of my uniform-wearing.

I did manage to suffer through a uniform phase when I was an LAPD beat cop, but as soon as I made detective, it was over.

When I joined the San Remo County Sheriff's Department, I defied convention and remained a plainclothes guy, thereby producing yet another bone of contention between my father and me.

"What do we know?" I asked Marsha.

"About Henry Carson?"

"Yes. Him."

Marsha opened her laptop and read aloud. "Henry Carson. Born, 1987. Montclair, New Jersey. Graduated Montclair High School, 2004. Earned a degree in Education at Fairleigh Dickinson University, 2008. Stayed on for one more year of graduate work. Taught American History at Columbia High School, Maplewood, New Jersey, for eight years. Became the Assistant Principal at Freedom High last year, where he's also on the coaching staffs of the baseball and swim teams."

"Personal?"

"Married Kimber Collins, Montclair, New Jersey, December 2017. No children. Both parents still living."

"Here?"

"Montclair."

"Any strangeness?"

Marsha looked up from her laptop. "Strangeness?"

"Anything weird?"

"Nothing apparent."

"The principal?"

"Julia Peterson," Kennerly said. "Who, by the way, eagerly awaits her audience with you."

"What do I need to know?"

"She's a cool customer. Claims to have had a good working relationship with the deceased. When pressed, she made mention of the fact they did little or no socializing. She's a no-nonsense type. Deadly serious."

"My kind of person. Forensics?"

"Nothing yet," Striar said. "I'm hoping for something by end of day."

"Shall we, Marsha?"

"No time like the present."

"So what are we waiting for?"

• • ● • •

We were ushered into Julia Peterson's office by her assistant, a nerdy-looking young man wearing an off-the-rack blue suit, the ill-fitting kind, likely part of a "buy one, get one free" promotion.

Ms. Peterson appeared to be in her mid-to-late thirties, a handsome woman, also in a blue suit, hers far better tailored than her assistant's. Her shoulder-length brown hair was streaked with red. Her wide brown eyes were lined with black. She wore a light dusting of blush and muted pink lipstick. She exuded the faint scent of Chanel Chance. Hers was a turned-up nose that wrinkled when she smiled.

Marsha and I wrestled ourselves into the not-so-comfortable hardwood armchairs that fronted her desk.

Her office was located just inside the main entrance of the school. It was painted light beige, boasting a pair of wood-framed picture windows that faced the street. A small conference table occupied one side of the room, across from her oversized desk. A large bookcase filled the wall behind her along with two wooden filing cabinets.

A framed picture adorned the wall behind the conference table, a copy of Edward Hopper's painting, *Nighthawks.*

I stared at it for a while, then murmured, "His most memorable work."

"Certainly his most popular," Ms. Peterson said. "The students cotton to it right away. A number of them comment on its inherent sense of loneliness. They identify with the feeling of isolation the picture engenders. It's an ice-breaker."

She briefly flashed a kind of *"Aren't I erudite?"* smile that lacked warmth.

"What can you tell us about Henry Carson?" Marsha asked.

Ms. Peterson shifted slightly in her upholstered armchair. "I was just now re-reading his performance reports. Everything points to his having done his job well. He's been here for two semesters. No complaints have been registered."

"And your personal connection with him?"

"Cordial. He was open and friendly. He seemed earnest and he performed his administrative duties successfully. From what I can glean, his extracurricular activities with the sports department also earned him kudos. The students seemed to like him. There's nothing in any of the files that leads me to believe he was a problem case."

"So, no apparent motives for his murder."

"None that I could discern."

"And you had no issues with him?"

"Issues?"

"There was nothing out of line that came to your attention regarding his performance here?"

"As I said, he was a well-regarded professional. In my experience, he was always courteous and considerate. He had charm and a kind of charisma. Everyone seemed to like him. I know I certainly did."

I stood. Marsha followed my lead.

"Thank you for your time, Ms. Peterson. We've just begun our investigation. It's possible we'll need to speak with you again."

"I understand. I'll be happy to assist in any way I can."

On our way out, we nodded to Julia Peterson's nerdy assistant, who flashed us a forlorn grin.

Once back at the station, we were joined by Al Striar.

"Forensics," he said. "Inconclusive. Especially as they relate to the knife. It appears to have been wiped. Lots of trace evidence around the office, but nothing fresh. Nothing to suggest any kind of scuffle."

"Opinion?"

"The killer was known to Mr. Carson. He or she gained easy access. I'm guessing the knife was a big surprise to him and that the killer acted swiftly and decisively before Carson had the chance or the inclination to defend himself. Killer knew the right place to plant the knife. Sliced the windpipe and ruptured the carotid artery. Death was pretty quick."

I sat quietly for several moments imagining the horrific manner in which Henry Carson died, which gave me the shivers. Then I said to Marsha Russo, "Let's ramp this thing up. Something's not jiving here."

"Meaning?"

"Somebody took this guy out. In his office. Someone known to him. Premeditated violence like that doesn't just happen. Somebody had a serious grievance. Let's find out what it was and who it affected deeply enough to warrant murder."

Chapter Four

Freedom, California, is a small, seaside community located in San Remo County, halfway between Santa Barbara and San Francisco. I was born and raised here.

Now I was living in a rented, not-quite-fully-furnished, two-bedroom condo that offered views of the Freedom Township foothills on one side and the Pacific Ocean on the other. It felt transient enough to satisfy my need for impermanence.

I studied criminal justice at John Jay University in New York City, and upon graduation, joined the Los Angeles Police Department.

I was immediately at home in L.A., in Hollywood, actually, totally dedicated to my work and to the nonconventional lifestyle of a resolute single, more intent upon hooking up than on settling down.

At six-three, thirty-one years old, physically fit and okay-looking, living in a universe that contained some of the most attractive women on the planet, I believed I was heading into what I would come to remember as the best years of my life. A fantasy that was cut short by my father's illness, the reality of which wiped out whatever wind was filling my sails.

Having been overwhelmingly re-elected to a third term as San Remo County Sheriff, he had pushed all of my buttons and persuaded me to move back to Freedom and become his Chief Deputy. I was to cover his back and ostensibly succeed him when he could no longer fulfill his duties as his ALS progressed.

It wasn't the job that attracted me. It was the father/son thing. We had never been close, Burton Steel, Senior, and me, B.S., Junior. He was a difficult man, guarded, dour, and emotionally unavailable.

During my time at Jay College, I had undergone a couple of years of psychoanalysis, which had a significant impact on me. When my father became ill and asked me to join him, I knew it would be the only chance I would have to deal with whatever unfinished business existed between us. So I returned to the nest. The nest I had come to wish I might flee at the earliest opportunity.

Communication with the old man had always been difficult. He had never been given to introspection. Now, facing near-certain death, he retreated even farther from self-examination. He was distracted and depressed. And angry.

He was still able to push my buttons, and at the same time, fill me with despair. I arrived in Freedom well-intentioned and eager for the challenge of deepening our relationship, only to be disillusioned and disappointed.

I often found myself angry, too, unable to capture his attention and fearful that whatever opportunity for closeness I had imagined we might achieve was no more than a pipe dream.

I was in my office, feet up, staring out the window, gazing at a darkening sky, mulling, when Marsha Russo knocked on my door.

Marsha was a robust woman of significant energy, a "shtarker," as my father called her, quick-witted and smart-mouthed.

"Problem," she said as she sat down heavily in front of my desk.

"What problem?"

"Kimber Collins Carson."

"The widow?"

"The widow."

"What about her?"

"She's gone."

"She's gone?"

"Stop repeating everything I say. Yes. She's gone. I phoned to set up an appointment and when the phone went unanswered, I drove out to her condo."

"Because?"

"Something didn't feel right. In any event, she wasn't there. Her car was in the garage and she wasn't home."

"So?"

"So I checked around a bit. Seems an Uber driver picked her up at around seven o'clock last evening and brought her to Freedom Field."

"And?"

"She took a shuttle to LAX, followed by a United flight to Newark."

"So she's left the state."

"She has. Yes."

"When you spoke with her yesterday, did you make mention of the fact she shouldn't leave the state?"

"She was so plotzed, it wouldn't have mattered what I mentioned to her."

"Plotzed?"

"Colloquialism for heavily sedated."

"Have you tried to reach her? Isn't she from New Jersey?"

"Montclair, actually. I phoned her parents' house. Twice."

"And?"

"She wouldn't take my call."

"But she was there."

"According to the man who answered the phone, she was."

I knew this didn't bode well, either for the widow or for me. I could already hear the District Attorney in my mind's ear and I fully expected to soon be on the receiving end of his displeasure.

Marsha interrupted my reverie. "What do you want to do, Buddy?"

"This raises her suspect profile."

"You think she did it?"

"I have no idea. I've never even spoken with her. I'm guessing she wanted to be with her family. But leaving town and not responding to your calls isn't good. I'll inquire as to the D.A.'s wishes."

"I'm sorry about this, Buddy."

"Me, too."

● ● ● ● ●

Assistant District Attorney Alfred Wilder picked up my call. "What do you want?" he said.

"And a good day to you, too, Skip."

"What is it, Buddy? I'm totally jammed here."

"I've got a conundrum."

"What?"

"A conundrum. You know, a problem. A quandary. A dilemma."

"I know the definition of conundrum, Buddy. Don't be such a jerk."

"Key figure in the Henry Carson murder case skipped town."

"Excuse me?"

"Carson's wife. She left the state."

"How could she have done that?"

"She took a local to LAX and a red-eye to Newark."

"Jesus, Buddy. Possible suspect in a murder case. She's not supposed to leave the state."

"That's why I'm calling."

"Lytell's not going to like this."

"Tell me something I don't know."

"Jesus, Buddy."

"You already said that."

"He's definitely not going to like this."

Rather than continuing to listen to Wilder's phumphering, I suggested, "How about you to get back to me on this, okay, Skip?"

I ended the call without waiting for his reply.

Chapter Five

Turns out the District Attorney was none-too-pleased, indeed. He returned my call within minutes. I put the call on speaker.

"Find her," he commanded. "She's just elevated herself into the prime suspect category. I want her back here."

"Seems she's gone home, Mike. Try to keep in mind she's in mourning."

"She had no business fleeing the state."

"She's a young woman whose husband was murdered. She's gone to be with her parents."

"And if it turns out she's the killer? If she ups and vanishes? Then what? We'll look like a pair of inept stupids, is what. That can't happen. You find her, Buddy. You arrest her and get her back here. Do I make myself clear?"

"You do."

"You're damned right, I do," he said. "Here, talk to Skip."

I could barely make out what he was saying as he handed the phone to A.D.A. Skip Wilder. He had covered the mouthpiece with his hand.

After several moments, Wilder came on the line. "I'll have the extradition papers drawn and cleared with the Jersey authorities."

Then he, too, covered the mouthpiece as he spoke to District Attorney Lytell. "What do you want him to charge her with?"

I couldn't make out Lytell's response. Then Wilder came back on the line. "Suspicion of murder."

"This is a whole lot of much ado about nothing, Skip."

"Perhaps you'd like to tell him that yourself."

"That's not all I'd like to tell him."

"Just do it, Buddy. Keep me in the loop."

I hung up and looked at Sheriff's Deputies John Kennerly and Marsha Russo, who were seated in front of my desk.

"That went well," Marsha snickered.

"Very entertaining," Kennerly said. "So, what now?"

"Book the flights. I'll talk with the locals and arrange for assistance when I get to Newark."

"You're going to make the trip?" Kennerly ventured.

"I am."

"Why?"

"You mean why am I the one who's going?"

"Yes."

"Cranky District Attorney?"

"You mean you're going because of Lytell?"

"It's actually a toss-up between him and the frequent flier miles."

Kennerly flashed me his dead-eyed stare and went on. "What if they try to stop you?"

"Her parents?"

Kennerly nodded.

"I'll deal with it."

"And if they lawyer her up?"

"The extradition agreement insures that the crime with which she's being charged is answerable in California."

"You think she did it?"

"You mean do I think she murdered her husband?"

"Yes."

"I haven't the foggiest."

Chapter Six

My flight landed at Newark Airport at first light, approximately four-fifty a.m. I was met at the gate by Detective Sergeant Deborah McGinness of the New Jersey State Police. She ushered me to an unmarked Chevrolet Caprice, which leapt away from the curb with the portable light bar the driver had planted on the roof flashing red.

The Sergeant, a middle-aged, short-haired, thin-lipped redhead, was constrained and reticent. We made the twenty-five-minute ride to Montclair in relative silence.

When we pulled up in front of Edith and Ed Collins' house on Conway Court, Sergeant McGinness and I stepped quickly to the front door and rang the bell.

After several moments, it was opened by a fifty-something gray-haired man in a bathrobe and slippers.

"What's all this?" he said as we stepped past him into a ranch-style residence that appeared to have been wrongly deposited amid a row of modest, suburban, tract houses.

The main entrance opened into the living room, a large family space whose main component was a monster-sized TV. To its left was a formal dining room, behind which was an eat-in kitchen that smelled of burnt toast and coffee that reminded me I hadn't yet had breakfast. A narrow hallway led to the bedrooms.

Sergeant McGinness produced the extradition papers. I handed him the arrest warrant. "Where is she?" I asked.

"I'm afraid I don't understand," the man said.

"Please tell me where I can find Kimber."

"She's in her room, of course."

"Point me to it."

The man hesitated.

"Now," I insisted.

He turned and headed up the hallway toward the bedrooms. I followed. He knocked on one of the four doors and then opened it a crack. I pushed past him.

Kimber Collins Carson was sitting up in bed, having obviously been awakened by the commotion. She rubbed the sleep from her eyes.

"You're under arrest," I told her.

Sergeant McGinness joined us. She read Kimber her rights, then instructed her to get dressed.

Mr. Collins and I stepped outside to wait. He glared at me. "She didn't do anything. She certainly didn't kill him."

"I'm sure she didn't, but she left California illegally, and by so doing, captured the District Attorney's attention. I'm under orders to take her back."

"But she just got here."

I shrugged.

Sergeant McGinness opened the door and led Kimber out of the bedroom. She was dressed in jeans and a gray hoodie, her hands cuffed behind her.

She stopped walking and looked at her father. "Tell Mom I'm sorry," she said.

When her father stepped toward her, her look stopped him in his tracks.

"I'm fine," she said.

I read alarm and concern in Ed Collins' tired eyes, which also reflected his anguish.

Sergeant McGinness hustled Kimber out of the house and into the Caprice. After offering my regrets to Mr. Collins, who nodded sadly, I hurriedly followed them.

We arrived back at the airport at six-thirty and were escorted by Sergeant McGinness onto the seven o'clock United flight to Los Angeles.

I thanked the Sergeant for her efforts. The doors closed and we were in the air heading home by seven-fifteen.

● ● ● ● ●

"Why?" Kimber Carson asked once we were airborne.

"For one thing, you left without our knowledge. Which rankled the District Attorney. A goodly number of familial homicides are committed by a spouse. You evaded a preliminary interview with one of my Deputies. You refused to accept her phone calls. You fled the state. And in doing so, made yourself the prime suspect."

"I didn't kill him."

"I sincerely hope that's the case, but you'll have to remain in custody until the State decides what to do with you."

She sat silently for a while, lost in thought.

I took notice of her for the first time. She was unconventionally attractive. Her boyishly styled, blond-streaked hair closely framed her slender face and called attention to her wide hazel eyes. She was gamine-like, possessing a slender beauty and a charismatic sensuality.

She noticed me staring. "Will you take the handcuffs off?"

"Will you create a disturbance?"

"I'm not a killer. I'm sorry I caused everyone so much trouble."

I removed the cuffs and she vigorously rubbed her wrists.

I watched her. "I'll need to put them back on you when we get to L.A."

We sat in silence for a while, she looking out the window, me perusing the in-flight magazine in search of a breakfast menu.

I wondered what it was like for her to have lived through the brutal killing of her husband and within a matter of days, to have become the prime suspect. Having worked homicide in L.A., I knew full well that anyone was capable of murder. Although she didn't strike me as a killer, it was possible the husband had done something awful enough to have rung her chimes.

"I was planning to divorce him."

I looked up at her. "Excuse me?"

"I was going to leave him. He wasn't the man I believed him to be when I married him."

"Because?"

"I mean he wasn't a wife beater or anything like that. But he had issues with being faithful."

"What kind of issues?"

"He was constantly around young people. Young girls mostly."

"And?"

"I think he was having sex with some of them."

"You think?"

A wrinkle of consternation crossed her face. "It's nothing I could prove. But he kept odd hours. Always involved with extracurricular activities of one kind or another. Sometimes he came home late. He went out at night. He lost interest in me."

"Interest how?"

"When we first got together, he couldn't keep his hands off me. Once we got to California, he rarely came near me."

"And you think it was because he was fooling around with his students?"

"I'm not saying that."

"What exactly are you saying?"

"Nothing I can prove."

"But something you suspect."

"Yes."

"What?"

"I think he may have been involved in some kind of sex ring."

"At the school?"

"Connected with the school."

"Involving students."

"That would be my guess."

"But you can't prove it."

"No."

She captured me in her steady gaze, her hazel eyes appraising me unwaveringly. I turned away and thought that, innocent or guilty, this was a woman scorned, one who might very well have been motivated to seek revenge.

"Will you help me?" she asked.

"Help you how?"

"I don't want to go to jail. I may be guilty of running away, but I didn't murder him."

"It's up to the District Attorney as to what charges will be filed."

"Murder?"

"More likely *suspicion of.*"

"I didn't do it."

"Fleeing the scene will influence the D.A.'s thinking."

"It wasn't deliberate. It's not like I left the country or vanished. I went home. You know, Mom and Dad? TLC? Who knew that wasn't allowed?"

The hint of a smile briefly appeared on her lips which I

tracked until it vanished. Then I said, "This can't be easy for you."

"Ditto," she responded.

Chapter Seven

"I don't believe she did it," I commented to A.D.A. Skip Wilder. We were sitting in his office, awaiting the arrival of District Attorney Michael Lytell.

"That's your considered opinion?"

"It is."

"I'll make note of it. In the meantime, she stays in County. No bail. She's already proven to be a flight risk."

"Come on, Skip. She didn't know she wasn't supposed to leave the state. No one told her."

"She acted willfully, with full knowledge that the Sheriff's Department was trying to reach her."

"This won't stick. Once she lawyers up, she'll be out in no time."

"Tell that to the D.A."

"Why do you think I'm here?"

He glared at me. I knew Skip from junior high school, when he was a nerdy kid with pimply skin. Like me. We were twelve. We hit it off almost immediately and soon became inseparable.

We had an uncanny knack for getting ourselves into trouble. Like the day we showed up for art class and found the teacher, Miss Safro, absent.

She had written the day's instructions on the blackboard.

We were to sketch any structure of our choosing and then color it in. A profusion of crayons were on her desk.

She had also inadvertently left a tube of Elmer's Glue-All beside the crayons. Which immediately caught our attention.

Rather than bother with the exercise of drawing and coloring, for some self-destructive reason, we chose instead to glue a number of the crayons onto the drawing table at which we were seated.

We arranged the crayons to look as if they had been haphazardly scattered on the table, but when you tried to pick one up, you couldn't.

Which reduced us to uncontrollable laughter.

At the end of the class, with still no Miss Safro, we exited the room, leaving the glued crayons behind.

It wasn't exactly brain surgery for Miss Safro to figure out it was Skip and me who had committed the crayon mayhem. Before the end of the school day, we were summoned to the Principal's office.

We sheepishly admitted our guilt. Our parents were notified and for the next four weeks, Skip and I were forbidden to have any contact with each other.

Except for when we inadvertently bumped into each other in the hallways. One glance and without so much as a word spoken, we would break into riotous laughter.

We've been friends ever since. Even now, in the face of a testy relationship between his boss and me, Skip and I remain close. They say the friends you make in your youth are the ones who remain truest throughout your lifetime.

There was a knock on Skip's door but before he could respond, it opened, revealing Michael Lytell, the portly D.A., along with Murray Kornbluth, the county's preeminent legal personage.

"Murray's representing the widow," Lytell exclaimed with a flourish as he and Kornbluth stormed into the office.

In typical Lytell fashion, he planted himself behind Wilder's desk, assuming the room's power position. They still tell the story of Thomas Baum, the San Remo County Chairman, who to this day refuses to stand whenever Lytell visits his office.

"That son of a bitch isn't going to sit in my chair," Baum tells anyone who questions why he remains seated whenever the District Attorney makes one of his grandiloquent entrances.

Murray Kornbluth, who grinned broadly when he spotted Lytell behind Wilder's desk, sat next to me in the vacant guest chair, leaving Wilder, who had risen deferentially when Lytell entered, forced to stand behind him, a frown darkening his visage as he watched the frenetic District Attorney peruse the chaotic crush of paperwork scattered atop Wilder's desk.

As I watched this little drama play itself out, I interrupted it. "I suppose this means I'll be releasing her."

Lytell shifted his focus to me. "Not until Judge Hiller says so."

"Which he most assuredly will," Kornbluth added.

The flashily dressed Murray Kornbluth was San Remo County's most celebrated attorney. Although he and D.A. Lytell were charter members of the exclusive Crestview Country Club, they were also longtime rivals at the Bar. Each kept a mental tab of how they fared against each other and the current tally showed them running neck and neck. I wanted no more of these two paragons of self-importance, so I stood and smiled at them both. "It's comforting to see the wheels of justice still greased and chugging."

"Always with the smart mouth, eh, Buddy?" Kornbluth said.

"In case it's of interest, there's little likelihood she did it."

"I told you he'd say that," Lytell said to Kornbluth.

"How long?" I asked.

"How long for what?" Lytell retorted.

"Until the illustrious judge rules?"

"He's already received the petition. He'll rule when he rules," Lytell said.

"Then I'll await further instruction," I said with a glance at Skip Wilder, who was still standing awkwardly behind his desk.

"Chair, Skip?" I said, pointing to the one I just vacated.

He glowered.

"Standing like that must be brutal," I chided. "It's always the legs that go first." I grinned at him and with nods to both the District Attorney and Murray Kornbluth, I hot-footed it out of there.

• ● ⬤ ● •

"I wonder how she hooked up with Kornbluth so fast," my father mused.

We were sitting on the sunporch of the family manse. He was on a lounge chair, swathed in a fleece blanket. He had lost weight and appeared gaunt. He was rubbing his hands together as if for warmth, even though the temperature was in the seventies.

"Had to have been at the arraignment," I surmised.

"You think a judicial staffer tipped him off?"

"As sure as we're sitting here, there's someone on the inside who's on his payroll."

"Any idea who?"

"Does it matter? He was bound to get this case one way or the other."

The old man nodded. "The investigation?"

"The widow told me she was planning to divorce him."

"Not an encouraging sign."

"For what it's worth, I don't think she did it."

"Because?"

"Coply intuition."

"And?"

"She believes he was involved in some kind of sexual she-nanigans."

"At the school?"

"Yes."

My father shook his head and stuffed his hands more deeply into the pockets of his ancient cardigan. Despite his visible discomfort, he enjoyed being informed as to the goings-on at the office.

As for me, I welcomed the chance to discuss business with him, to refocus his attention on something other than his illness. It allowed us to share a kind of forced intimacy, a chance to be close, an opportunity to permit the conversation to camouflage his terror, which lurked beneath the surface like an unseen predator, poised and ready to strike at any moment.

"Does the unholy trinity know about the so-called sexual shenanigans?" he asked.

"You mean Lytell, Kornbluth, and Judge Hiller?"

"Yeah. Them."

"Kornbluth, maybe. But I don't believe the others do."

"You're going to inform them?"

"Not yet."

"Because?"

"I don't know for sure it's true."

"But you think it is?"

"I don't know, Dad. I'm at the starting line. I'll let you know more as soon as I have some concrete information."

An eerie silence engulfed us. The old man began rubbing his hands again, a forlorn look appearing on his tired-looking face. "I feel like shit, Buddy."

"I'm sorry."

"I don't have any motivation."

"You can't be expected to."

"Tell that to my constituency."

As I caught him ebbing into self-pity, I did my best to steer him away from it.

"Your constituency adores you. They're solidly in your corner."

"Says you."

"You bet, says me. This thing you have ebbs and flows. Hang in, Burton. You still have a lot of good days in front of you."

"You think?"

"I know."

At last he flashed me a smile. "From your mouth to God's ear."

Chapter Eight

The boys were first up. I was in the stands of the Freedom High School pool house watching the swim team practice.

Situated in an extension of the steel and glass gymnasium that had been donated by a wealthy local, the vast, temperature-controlled edifice was home to an Olympic-size swimming pool, surrounded on all sides by bleachers.

Oversized windows ringed the top tier of the building, bathing the interior in natural light. Stadium-type lighting fixtures illuminated the pool at night.

They were swimming freestyle, all eight lanes of the pool occupied by slender young men, each with significant upper body musculature and beefy legs. Several similar-looking youths sat on the sidelines, all wearing skimpy Speedos with large white bath towels draped around their shoulders, intently watching.

A dozen young women wearing tight-fitting, one-piece bathing suits, also sat raptly watching and occasionally chattering among themselves.

After a while, one of the coaches blew his whistle and the swimmers made their way to the near end of the pool, where a circle formed around him.

"Okay, okay," the coach shouted over the din. "That's it for today, boys. Girls, you're up."

The boys climbed out of the pool and eight girls took their places at the head of each lane. The whistle shrieked and the girls dove into the water and began swimming laps.

A coach holding a clipboard looked in my direction. He handed the clipboard to one of his associates and climbed the bleacher steps to where I was seated. "Sheriff Steel," he said.

"Fred," I answered.

Fred Maxwell had been on the Freedom High School faculty for as long as I could remember. In addition to coaching the swim team, he was also the head of the Athletic Department, a gruff, take-no-prisoners type of executive, well into his sixties, widely regarded as a good guy.

He was red-faced in a way that suggested he might be a drinker. He wore scruffy sweats that matched the color of his thinning gray hair. A pair of horn-rimmed, thick-lensed eyeglasses hung on a chain around his neck.

He was more than just a coach; he had been a longtime source of encouragement and support for young men and women who were just coming of age. For decades he had helped ease anxieties and prop up delicate egos. He was a local institution. He planted himself on the row of benches in front of me and sighed. "How's he doing?"

"As well as can be expected."

"ALS?"

I nodded.

"You'll send him my regards."

"He'll be pleased."

"Shame about Hank," Maxwell said.

"Hank?"

"Carson. He was a decent man."

"You worked with him?"

"I did. He was great with the kids. He wasn't completely confident about the mechanics, but what he didn't know, he made up for in enthusiasm."

"Any reason for someone to do him harm?"

"I've been thinking about it, Buddy. I know he was close to a lot of the kids and, knowing teenagers as I do, they all tend to be fickle. But not when it came to Hank. He was definitely a great favorite."

"Which students was he close to?"

"Excuse me?"

"You said he was close to a lot of the kids. Which ones?"

"Forgive me if I sound like Sarah Palin here," he smiled. "All of them."

"He was close to all of them?"

"Equally. I can't really single out any of them as being closer than any other. But then, I suppose, I wouldn't really know. He spent time with team members outside of practice. Sometimes he took kids for dinners or on excursions."

"In groups or individually?"

"Both, I guess."

"But you don't know."

"I suppose I don't. Not exactly. But if you talk with any of the kids, I'm sure they'll fill you in."

"Which of the kids?"

"Well, the captains, for certain. Bobby Siegler for the boys. Chrissie Lester for the girls. They'll likely point you in the right direction."

I nodded. "Thanks for this, Fred. I'm at the starting line here, and I may have more questions later on."

"Just holler, Buddy. I'm always available."

Chapter Nine

Bobby Siegler stepped out of the locker room carrying a backpack and a smartphone into which he was punching a series of numbers. His hair was still wet.

"Mr. Siegler," I said.

He stopped and looked hard at me.

"Do I know you?"

"Buddy Steel. Deputy Sheriff, San Remo County."

"Sheriff?"

"Yes."

"Is this about Coach Carson?"

"Do you have time for a few questions?"

He snapped off his phone. "Sure."

We found a bench in front of the gymnasium. He dropped his backpack on it and sat. He pointed me to the space beside him. "How may I help?"

"Well, for openers, what can you can tell me about Mr. Carson?"

His brow furled slightly as he thought about what he might want to say. He was a handsome young man, with blond hair shorn tight to his head. Although small, he possessed a startling physique. He had on a tight-fitting Lacoste t-shirt worn over a pair of jeans that were stylishly ripped at the knees. He had six-pack abs and highly developed arms. "He was very kind to me," he said.

"In what way?"

Siegler's thoughts turned inward and he answered hesitatingly, shyly, parsing his words self-consciously as if muscling his way through something painful.

"I've always been devoted to swimming. Growing up, my parents couldn't get me out of the pool. But when I showed up for tryouts, I was the smallest kid here. And I didn't really know any of the others. So I was kind of standing alone. Nobody had much interest in me."

He stared at me intently as though he was weighing the effect his words were having and, more importantly, whether I was being judgmental.

After several moments, I guess he found me acceptable and went on. "But Coach Hank, he stepped right up and introduced himself. He looked me over and asked what I thought were my strengths and weaknesses. When I told him I was a diver, he brightened right up and walked me over to the board.

"'*Let's see what you got*,' he said. '*Don't hold back*.'" So suddenly everybody stopped what they were doing and stood watching me. But I wasn't nervous or anything. I had practiced my dives so many times I could do them blindfolded. I was prepared to do ten of them, but by the time I reached dive six, the kids were cheering.

"Coach took me under his wing and I've sort of considered him like a big brother ever since."

"In what ways did he take you under his wing?"

"In a lot of ways. He wasn't only interested in me as a diver. He helped with my schoolwork. If I was uncertain about things, he would ask me about them and advise me."

"What kind of things?"

"Pretty much everything. Things to do with my family. My friends. Stuff like that.

"Personal stuff."

"Yes. That's right."

"Did he ask about you and girls?"

Again he stared at me, but this time I could feel the window into his thoughts rapidly closing. He became guarded, uncomfortable, choosing his words more cautiously. "He was always helpful."

"With girls?"

"With everything."

That statement concluded our interview. He regarded me coolly, then stood, picked up his backpack and slung it over his shoulder. "I gotta go. My parents will start to worry if I'm late."

I stood, too. "Thanks for being so frank. You've been very helpful."

He was now in a rush to get away from me. "Good luck with finding the guy who did this. I can't tell you how sad I am about it."

"Guy?"

"Excuse me?"

"You said, the *guy* who did it. Why a guy?"

"No reason. I guess I've been thinking that the person who did it was a guy."

"I see. Well, in any event, thanks again."

"You bet," he said and hurried away.

I watched him hightail it away, musing on what it was about the interview that had raised my hackles. He was hiding something and I couldn't put my finger on what it was. But I'd surely be making it my business to find out.

Chapter Ten

"He's not letting her out," Marsha Russo told me when I showed up at the office.

"What do you mean, he's not letting her out?"

I flopped down onto my chair and took a deep breath.

"Judge Hiller," Marsha continued. "He set bail at ten million dollars, which the family can't come up with."

"What did he do that for?"

"Opinion?"

"If need be."

"I think he wanted to stick it to Murray Kornbluth."

"Because?"

"Because somewhere there's a scorecard. A balance sheet. Kornbluth knows it. The D.A. knows it. And it serves to influence the judge."

"So her imprisonment was dictated by a three-legged scorecard?"

"I never said that."

"But you implied it."

"I did. But I never said it."

"Aren't we the semanticist?"

"Whatever that means."

"So, where is she?"

"Still in a County Courthouse holding cell."

"Jesus."

"What did you learn at the school?" she asked.

"That seldom is heard a discouraging word."

"Meaning?"

"Everyone thinks he was a saint."

"Everyone?"

"Except for the widow."

"Who thinks…?"

"He wasn't the man she married."

"So, now what?"

"The investigation continues."

"And?"

"Murray Kornbluth appeals."

"And?"

"I don't know, Marsha. This murder has given me a roaring headache."

"Take two aspirin and call me in the morning."

● ● ● ● ●

She was the only occupant. The other seven cells were empty. It was a depressing place, having been hastily constructed in the basement of the County Courthouse as a makeshift holding facility for prisoners in transit.

She was lying on a metal-framed cot that was, along with a metal chair, the cell's only furniture. And there was a sink and a toilet.

She looked up when I entered. "Is it you who's responsible for my being here?"

"Not hardly."

"Why, then? I can't get a reasonable answer from Mr. Kornbluth."

She was still dressed in the jeans and hoodie she wore on the flight back to Los Angeles. She was disheveled and dismayed.

"Didn't anyone bring you fresh clothing?"

"Does it look like I'm wearing fresh clothing?"

She was doing her best to remain calm and under control, but it was clear that beneath the surface, she was seething. Unkempt and uncertain, her world had turned upside-down and she was shaken by it.

"You didn't answer my question," she said.

"I don't really know. I'm surprised he wasn't able to get you out. Or why bail was set so high. I'll make it my business to look into it."

"Why?"

"Why what?"

"Why would you do that?"

"Because I believe you."

"That I didn't do it?"

"Yes."

"It's nice to know someone believes me."

I smiled. "Sometimes the ways and means of a small town get in the way of justice."

"Which means?"

"Politics."

She didn't speak.

"What do you need?" I asked.

"Excuse me?"

"Clothing. Supplies. What do you need?"

"Why do you want to know?"

"I'll arrange to get them for you."

"You'd do that?"

"Yes."

"Why would you?"

"I don't know, Kimber. But I will."

"And you'll speak to Murray Kornbluth?"

"Yes."

She didn't say anything for a while. I watched as a whole panoply of emotions flashed in her hazel eyes. Then she turned to me. "It's nice."

"What is?"

"That you're kind to me. You're the only one."

"We'll get through this."

"We?"

"A figure of speech."

Chapter Eleven

When she stepped outside and saw me standing there, Chrissie Lester turned and walked in the opposite direction. I waited a few seconds and then followed.

If she was aware of me behind her, she didn't show it. She kept walking, heading for the school parking lot. When she reached a maroon Prius, she used her remote to unlock it and was about to step inside when she finally acknowledged my presence. "Why are you following me?"

"You're Chrissie Lester."

"What of it?"

"I'm Deputy Sheriff Steel."

"Okay."

"Do you have a few moments?"

"Not really. I have to get home."

"I'll only take a tiny bit of your time."

She sighed theatrically and stood staring at me with one hand planted firmly on her hip. She was a plain-looking young woman, not particularly attractive. She wore a gray sleeveless sweatshirt over extremely short cropped jeans that revealed a good deal of leg and a glimpse of the bottom of her shapely behind. She was self-possessed, confident, and overflowing with attitude.

"If you must," she said.

I flashed her my sincerest smile, an effort to win her with my incalculable charm. "What can you tell me about Henry Carson?"

"The coach?"

"Yes."

"Well, for one thing, he's dead."

She stared at me in smug anticipation of my response. I could sense her disappointment when I chose to remain silent. At last she spoke. "I didn't have much to do with him."

"Wasn't he one of your coaches?"

"Mostly he coached the boys. We girls kept our distance from him."

"Why is that?"

"I don't know if I want to go into this."

"Go into what?"

"He was somewhat of a polarizing person."

"Meaning?"

"He was into separating us."

"I don't understand."

"You were either a Coach Hank person, or you weren't."

"What was the distinction?"

"Your looks."

"Meaning?"

"You were either good-looking or you weren't."

"And if you weren't?"

"He had nothing to do with you."

"What if you were good-looking?"

"He was your new best friend."

"And you?"

"Clearly, he had nothing to do with me."

"Aren't you the captain?"

"I am."

"How could he have nothing to do with you?"

She dropped her hand-on-hip pose and leaned heavily against the Prius. Some of the air appeared to go out of her. Her attitude softened. She exhibited teenage vulnerability, an uncertainty that made her more accessible and even a bit friendly.

She went on. "Maybe I'm not making myself clear. If you were a Coach Hank Girl, you received special privileges. Sometimes he'd take you to Gruning's ice cream parlor after practice. He talked you up to your teachers. Some girls he'd even invite out to dinner."

"So you weren't included in any of his extracurricular activities?"

"Never."

"Even as the captain."

"Whatever contact we had, me being the captain and all, he was cordial and polite. But he wasn't warm and charming."

"Which he was to the so-called Coach Hank Girls?"

"Exactly."

"Did you ever speak with your teammates about this?"

"All the time."

"And?"

"The good-looking girls shrugged their shoulders as if being a Coach Hank Girl was nothing special."

"And the others?"

"Like me, you mean?"

"You know, Chrissie, I have no interest in passing judgment on your Coach Hank-Girl qualifications, but to me you're quite nice-looking. You're articulate and clearly smart. Assets that are every bit as important as your looks. More so, even."

"Well, he didn't think so."

"So what?"

"So me and some of the others were left standing by the side of the road when Coach and his cadre went roaring off into the sunset."

"Did any members of his cadre ever complain about Coach Hank?"

"Complain?"

"You know. Did he ever get out of line with them? Did he ever come on to any of them?"

"I wouldn't know. If he did, no one ever said anything to me about it."

"What do you think?"

"About whether or not he was a lech?"

"Something like that. Yes."

Now she looked at me with contempt—as if she had just come to the conclusion I was a waste of her time. An annoyance. Like she was the wrong tree for me to be barking up.

"What I think doesn't mean squat. If you want to know about what went on between Coach and his girls, go ask them. Are we done now?"

Clearly, she was. She glanced at her watch and began fidgeting, anxious to get as far away from me as possible. She asked again, "Are we?"

"I suppose we are."

I reached inside my shirt pocket and pulled out one of my cards. I scribbled my cell phone number on the back and handed it to her. "If you think of anything else, call me."

She took the card and briefly glanced at it, then at me. She folded it in half, dropped it into her bag, got into the Prius, and drove off.

The Coach Hank Girls, I muttered to myself. I didn't like the sound of it. What it portended. What bothered me more was the disparate impacts he seemed to have had on Bobby

Siegler and on Chrissie Lester. That there existed a polarity of criteria. Some were in and others were clearly out. Attractive was in. Unattractive was out.

Which bothered me even more.

Chapter Twelve

"Why would you care?"

"I don't know, Dad. That's the same question she asked."

"She being the widow?"

"Yes."

"So? Why would you care?"

"I guess because I don't believe she should be in jail. And I take some responsibility for that."

"Because no one told her not to leave town?"

"Yes."

"Wouldn't that be obvious?"

"Not necessarily to a young woman whose husband was just brutally murdered, who was sedated, and who wasn't thinking clearly."

The Sheriff was making one of his rare appearances at the courthouse and was seated in his office with nothing much to do except show the flag, so to speak. Staff members and Deputies stopped in to pay their respects. They lifted his spirits.

"Judge Hiller, right?" he asked.

"Yes."

"Okay. I'll talk to him."

"Were he to lower the bail to a more manageable number, her parents could likely post it. Be good if he could do it right away. She's still in some kind of emotional shock. Being in jail is tough on her."

"I'll do my best."

I stood and stepped over to him. I squeezed his shoulder and rested my hand gently on his cheek for a moment.

"Don't go getting all soft and mushy on me, Buddy," he said.

"I'll try my best."

When I reached the door, he called to me. "You're not interested in this woman, are you?"

"Interested?"

"You're not doing this because you're attracted to her? Like you were with the last one."

"The last one?"

"The Reverend's sister."

"Why would you say a thing like that?"

"You know what I'm getting at, Buddy. Best not to shit where you eat."

I stared at him. "You know, Regina has a point."

"About?"

"About what a profane son of a bitch you are."

He flashed me his most sardonic grin. "And proud of it, too."

The conversation with my father was unsettling. It's true I might have stepped over the line when I became involved with Maggie de Winter, the sister of the con-artist preacher I had been investigating when we met.

I keep telling myself it was inadvertent. A sudden, irresistible itch that I scratched before realizing what I was doing.

But psychoanalysis had taught me that this type of self-justification was bullshit. Unconsciously, I had set myself up for a fall and, while I became mired in self-pity for a moment when it ended, I knew damn well it was doomed right from the start. We were both emotionally unavailable, but despite that, I had lurched forward with un-evolved blindness.

"Be wary of participating in a conspiracy against yourself," my shrink always told me.

Which is what I had not done with Maggie. And I paid a price for it.

I vowed not to succumb to my feral instincts. Kimber Carson was damaged goods and taking advantage of her vulnerability, although tempting, was another way of emotionally shooting myself in the foot. I would do what I could to help her because I had a measure of guilt over her having left town. But as for hooking up with her, no way, no how.

My musings were interrupted by the insistent intrusion of my cell phone. "What?"

"You need to see something," Johnny Kennerly barked back at me.

"What do I need to see?"

"It's beyond description. You have to see it for yourself."

"Where?"

"Temple Israel."

"When?"

"Rabbi Weiner is waiting for you."

"And you?"

"I'm with him."

The call served to postpone my musings about the possibility that I might once again be on the threshold of behaving neurotically. It couldn't have come at a better time.

With a sigh of relief, I said, "I'm on my way."

Chapter Thirteen

"At least it's not anti-Semitic," Rabbi Herbert Weiner proclaimed.

We were standing in front of the Temple Israel Recreational Center, a postmodern glass-and-concrete structure whose soaring white walls were now covered in graffiti. Giant red upper and lower case letters had been spray-painted on a sky-blue background. The letters, when read in sequence, spelled *ROBBER XMAS*.

"How on Earth was he able to access the wall in the first place?" Johnny Kennerly pondered.

"It appears that the back gate had been left unlocked," the Rabbi said. "Not an unusual occurrence."

"Because?" I inquired.

"Complacency, I suppose. We've never been vandalized before, so over time we stopped handing out keys and just closed the gate without locking it."

"This doesn't look like the first time this artist has left his calling card. It's a very confident job," Johnny stated.

"But it's a first for Freedom," I said. "We haven't seen any graffiti in this town."

The Rabbi frowned. "I hope it's not the start of a scourge."

Herb Weiner had been Chief Rabbi of Temple Israel since its

inception in the late nineteen eighties. He was a scraggy man, prone to wearing rumpled black suits. He had a well-tended salt-and-pepper beard but his once-flourishing curly black hair had both thinned and grayed. He suffered from chronic back pain which slowed his movements and affected his posture. "What do you think Robber Xmas signifies?"

"Could be anything. Taggers love to sign their so-called artwork. Makes them feel important. We'll check to see if there are any persons named Christmas listed in the county. Probably be a good idea to re-visit your decision not to lock the gate. Just in case it is an act of anti-Semitism."

"Will do."

I noticed that the Rabbi was rubbing his lower back.

His face was a portrait of discomfort. I attempted to distract him. "We'll also check the hardware and paint stores for any large recent spray-paint purchases. I'm not hopeful because, unless the tagger was a rank amateur, it's not likely his supplies were purchased in the same town whose buildings he was planning to deface."

"Or her," the Rabbi offered.

"Or her," I agreed.

A smile served to relieve some of his suffering. "You'll let me know what you uncover?"

"Absolutely. Be it him or her."

● ● ● ● ●

Johnny went off on his quest to identify the tagger. No sooner had I revved up my cruiser and pulled away from the temple than my cell phone rang again.

"We may be witnessing the start of an epidemic," Marsha Russo said when I picked up the call.

"What's that supposed to mean?"

"Binder and Klein Outlet."

"What about it?"

"Big warehouse."

"I know it."

"Graffiti."

"Painted on the warehouse?"

"Yup."

"I'm on my way."

The Binder and Klein Furniture Outlet was a brick-and-mortar box store on Highway 16, the route from Freedom to White Sands. It, along with several other giant stores, formed the equivalent of an outlet mall row along the heavily trafficked stretch of freeway between the two beach communities.

I was greeted by Harry Binder. He'd been standing in front of the store, puzzling over how he was going to get rid of the gigantic mess of graffiti that now desecrated the entire wall of the building that faced Highway 16.

"What a mess," Harry said to me as I stood beside him taking stock of the damage. "Who would do such a thing?"

"Likely a tagger who calls himself Robber Xmas." I pointed to the lower case letters that spelled that name.

Harry Binder stood shaking his head. "It's a plague. Everywhere you go. Wherever you look these days you see graffiti. In doorways. On storefronts. On roadway fencing. And now Freedom. And who is it cleans this crap up? Who pays for it? It's become so prevalent that the authorities appear to have simply given up on trying to control it. The loonies have taken over the bin."

"Not exactly."

Binder looked at me. "Which means?"

"They're not going to win the Freedom battle."

"Yeah, well good luck with that one, Buddy."

Chapter Fourteen

Each new day brought another complaint about graffiti having appeared overnight on buildings, in parking lots, on monuments, roadways, overpasses... and as Harry Binder had pronounced, pretty much everywhere.

More and more signatures were now adorning freshly painted, sizable, and hideous-looking wall illustrations. Portraits of the likes of Johnny Depp and Lady Gaga had been elaborately spray-painted in a variety of colors on once-pristine walls, situated on both public and private property.

Landscapes of moon craters and subterranean cities stood side-by-side with walls full of ghastly cartoon characters and terrifyingly deformed gargoyles. Every conceivable surface was a potential target for vandals who considered themselves street artists, some of whom had now come to roost in Freedom.

Where they came from and why they chose this particular township was a mystery. They sprouted up overnight and the time had arrived to be more aggressive about apprehending and punishing them.

The Freedom Town Council occupied a neo-Classical building from the nineteen fifties. I made my way through the ornate lobby and hurried to my appointment with Council President Helena Madison.

President Madison had graduated magna cum laude from Stanford Law School and, before relocating to Freedom, was a partner in the prestigious Los Angeles branch of the Wincor, Harris, and Colton Law Firm.

When an unexpected death vacated the office of Freedom Council President, she was persuaded to run for the position and won in a landslide.

She stood to greet me when I entered her large yet modestly appointed office. She was nearly as tall as I, dressed in a black pantsuit, her unruly mop of pitch-black hair now tied in a severe bun. She was a woman of color who had also made a reputation as one of California's leading female athletes, a basketball standout at both Hollywood High and Stanford.

A mile-wide smile adorned her handsome face as she stepped out from behind her desk and gave me a welcoming hug. She pushed away from me and gave me the once-over.

"Not too bad for a geezer," she pronounced.

"Ditto," I said.

She laughed and kissed me lightly on both cheeks. We made ourselves comfortable in the sitting area overlooking the small park that stood in front of the Council building.

She took a sip from a bottle of mineral water. "Okay, Buddy. First I have to know how he's doing."

"It's tough for him, Helena. His faculties are diminishing. He fights, but it's not a battle he'll win in the long run."

"I'm sorry."

"I'm sure he'd welcome a phone call. He's very proud of you. He brags about you as if you were his second daughter."

She smiled. "Must be nice for him having you around."

"I hope so. But it's not always a two-way street."

"Your fault, no doubt."

"No doubt."

Helena Madison and I had met at the basketball court

adjacent to Muscle Beach in Venice, California. She was then a young attorney and I a police recruit. We found ourselves playing on opposite sides of a pick-up game which, on that particular day, also included former Laker greats James Worthy and A.C. Green.

Helena was teamed with Big Game James, I with A.C. None of us had anticipated a game of much intensity, but it was a beautiful Los Angeles Sunday, a large crowd was watching, and we played as if there was something at stake.

I was guarding Helena, who began the festivities by introducing me to both of her sharp elbows, which would dog me for the entire game. At first I was reluctant to mix it up with a woman, but within the first few minutes of the game, she made me forget that fact by bumping, grabbing, and generally harassing me from one end of the court to the other.

At half-time, she sidled over to me and shoved her hip against mine and in the doing, pushed me slightly off-balance. "Nice to meet you."

I resisted the urge to shove her back.

"I'll be thinking of you tonight when I'm applying the heat packs," she said.

"Perhaps you'd like some cheese to go with that whine."

"A wise guy, huh?"

"If you think heat packs are exclusively your domain, perhaps you'd like to take a closer look at my thigh?"

"Not in this lifetime, big boy. I just wanted to warn you that I'm a second half girl."

"Meaning?"

"Wait." She winked at me and ambled over to her bench. Once there, she turned back to me.

I flashed her a lopsided grin and rubbed my extended middle finger along the side of my nose.

She glared at me for a moment, then burst out laughing. We've been friends ever since.

When she married and moved to Freedom, she and her husband, Gregory, stayed at my father's house until they found a place of their own. My stepmother was godmother to their first-born daughter, Vanessa. My dad was godfather to their first-born son, Greg, Jr., or Little Greg, as he was currently called, despite the fact he was already tall for his age.

"So, what did I do to warrant this visit?" she asked.

"Graffiti."

"What graffiti?"

I told her of the developing crisis. "I'm going to have to step up my efforts to wrangle this puppy, and I need your help."

"How?"

"The current penalty for defacement of property is a thirty-dollar fine."

"So?"

"I want to petition the Council to raise it to twenty-five hundred."

"Twenty-five hundred dollars? That's some fine."

"And that would be just for openers. First offense."

"And for subsequent offenses?"

"Thirty-five hundred for the second. And a bump of a thousand dollars for every additional one."

"You know what, Buddy," she mused, "I'm beginning to think you may be off your rocker."

"There's more."

"What more could there be?"

"Thirty days in jail."

"You're kidding?"

"Have you looked at what's going on here?"

"At the graffiti?"

"Yes."

"I can't say I have."

"Then I'd like to arrange a tour. For you and the other

Council members. I'd like you to see where we stand now, and then again in a week from now. If we don't create meaningful penalties, we're sunk."

"When do you want this tour to take place?"

"Tomorrow."

She sat silently for a while. "Let me take it up with the others. I'll get back to you."

"When?"

"This is going to be a hard-sell, Buddy."

"When?"

"I hope you realize what a pain in the ass you are."

I stood. "I'm counting on you, Helena."

"This isn't going to be any kind of a slam dunk."

I grinned at her and rubbed my nose with my extended middle finger.

"Get some new material," she said with a laugh.

Chapter Fifteen

Johnny Kennerly had been my father's first hire when he became Sheriff. Not exactly a hire. During his junior year at Roosevelt High in North Freedom, after his class had toured the station and my father had given them a lecture on police work, Johnny started hanging around, offering to do odd jobs. He expressed his interest in law enforcement and, when the Sheriff offered him a summer internship, he jumped at it.

They became close, Johnny and my father, who saw him as the son he wished I was, a son who sought his counsel and was influenced by his opinions and his wisdom. He earned a special place in the Sheriff's heart. Burton, Senior, came to know Johnny's family—his single parent mother and younger sister.

Impressed and proud that Johnny was a high school honors student, my father used his influence to gain him admittance to Cal Poly, the San Luis Obispo branch of California Polytechnic State University, and paid the tuition out of his own pocket. Upon Johnny's graduation, my father hired him and, following a couple of years of general police work, elevated him to Deputy status.

When the old man was diagnosed with ALS and I joined the department as his Chief Deputy, Johnny went out of his way to put me at my ease. He innately understood the complicated nature of my relationship with my father, and he made a point of being a friend to us both.

Although Johnny and I did our best to conceal it, there existed an unspoken tension between us—more so since I'd returned to Freedom. He had been the favored probationer. I was the prodigal son. As a result, a measure of uneasiness permeated our association.

"They're like cockroaches," Johnny said to me over burgers and fries at Marley's Malt Shoppe. "They come out at night and move around unseen by human eyes."

"How poetic of them."

"I'm serious, Buddy. No one claims to ever have seen any of these taggers. In the morning, when people discover their handiwork, they're shocked and surprised."

"That will definitely have to change."

"Have you any suggestions as to how we can effect such a change?"

"We outsmart them."

"Oh, that old ruse."

"You got anything better?"

"Have you?"

"Let me get back to you on that."

I was sitting in my office with my feet up, watching the rain cascade down the window, when Marsha Russo strolled in and parked herself on one of the two visitor chairs in front of the desk.

Without turning around, I said, "What?"

"You're so cordial. No wonder I'm awed in your presence."

"What is it you want, Marsha?"

"Some analysis."

"See a shrink."

"Not that kind of analysis. Investigative analysis."

I removed my feet from the windowsill, whirled my chair around, and faced her. "There's no rest for the weary."

"Perhaps you should try another line of work."

"What kind of investigative analysis?"

"The Chrissie Lester kind."

I leaned closer and said, "Did you know there was such a thing as a Hank Girl?"

"That's what she told you?"

"Some girls were and some girls weren't."

"What was the criteria?"

"Looks."

"Sounds sexist to me."

"To Chrissie, also. She was reluctant to talk about it."

"What does that tell you?"

"I don't really know yet. It appears to play into the reasons Kimber Carson gave for wanting to leave the guy. But it's too early to jump to any conclusions."

"You're thinking sex ring, aren't you?"

I admired the way Marsha retained information. If she didn't exactly have a photographic memory, what she had was the closest thing to it. She had been at my father's side for nearly his entire reign as Sheriff. In fact, her service began with his predecessor who had hired her as a dispatcher. But once my father took charge, he recognized her talent and bumped her up to the command unit as Staff Captain.

In her early forties at the time, divorced with a grown daughter out of the house, Marsha welcomed the unexpected promotion and took the job seriously. Her duties were far-ranging but mostly she kept track of whatever was going on at any particular time and was the Department watch dog when it came to administration, assignments, and protocols.

She was an inherently curious person and frequently adopted the role of Inquisitor General. Which she was now playing.

She and I had bonded early on, a bond that had grown stronger since my return to Freedom. She took great pleasure in ragging on me, but because of her good-heartedness, I gladly accepted the role of victim but never failed to seek the opportunity to strike back.

"There's no proof of the existence of a sex ring. There's only Kimber's supposition," I told her.

"Where there's smoke?"

"Smoke in the form of?"

"Hank Girls. I don't like the sound of that."

"Perhaps it would be beneficial were you to have chats with a few of the Not Hank Girls. Gauge the level of their resentment. See if any of them might reveal something untoward to another woman."

"My, aren't we the wordsmith this morning?"

"Would the question '*Why are you still here?*' have any resonance with you?"

She stood. "Not that I can readily say. But I'll mull on it and get back to you." Without so much as a glance in my direction, she strolled out of the office.

Chapter Sixteen

Wilma Hansen, the longtime dispatcher and occasional phone operator, buzzed me. "Your father on line two."

"Isn't he in the building?"

"He is."

"And he wants me on the phone?"

"Hey, I just work here. I don't do family counseling. Are you going to take the call or should I tell him to go shove it?"

"I'll take it. Thank you for your kindness."

"No problem."

I picked up the call. "Your presence is requested," the Sheriff said.

"Where?"

"Judge Hiller's office. He, the D.A., and Murray Kornbluth are about to decide your lady friend's fate."

"My lady friend?"

"You know, the widow."

"You mean Kimber Carson?"

"Yes. Her."

"My lady friend?"

"Figure of speech."

"You know something, Dad, not only are you profane, you're also perverse."

"Thank you."

"That wasn't meant as a compliment."

● ● ● ● ● ●

Judge Franklin Hiller's office was located in the County Courthouse and the hearing was just starting when I stepped into his chambers.

Beleaguered by neatness, Hiller's office was always immaculate. It wasn't out of character for him to saunter over to a bookcase in the middle of a meeting to straighten an offending, ill-placed volume or even do a little dusting.

Wearing a blue-checked suit and a red bow tie, he stared daggers at me when I entered. The meeting had already begun and I was late. "Good of you to join us," he said with the slightest edge of annoyance in his voice.

I nodded sheepishly and gazed briefly at Michael Lytell and Murray Kornbluth, both of whom eyed me warily.

We were seated in front of the judge's desk in the cavernous, dark-wood and rich leather office that abutted his courtroom. Lytell and Kornbluth were in the two stuffed armchairs. A Bentwood chair had been pulled over for me.

"There's been a motion to reduce bail for Kimber Carson," Hiller plowed forward. "Are there any objections to this motion?"

Michael Lytell raised his hand.

The judge noticed him. "Mr. Lytell?"

"As I said at the initial hearing, I regard Mrs. Carson as a flight risk and believe she should be held without bail."

Judge Hiller turned to Murray Kornbluth, who ventured, "She's a grieving widow, Your Honor, who had not been informed she wasn't permitted to leave the state. She returned to her family home in New Jersey to mourn with them. She's not a flight risk. She's not a murderer. She's a young widow who suffered a grievous loss."

The judge then turned to me. "Have you anything to add to this, Mr. Steel?"

"I concur with Mr. Kornbluth. In the aftermath of the discovery of Henry Carson's body, I was derelict in my responsibility to inform Mrs. Carson she couldn't leave the state. Accountability for what she did belongs to me. And I apologize to the Court for my failure to properly execute my duties."

"Thank you for your frankness," Judge Hiller said. "Apology accepted."

He turned his attention to the District Attorney. "Mr. Lytell?"

"My statement stands."

After several moments of silence, Judge Hiller looked at us and gently banged his gavel. "Bail for Mrs. Carson is hereby reduced to five thousand dollars."

"Five thousand dollars," Lytell said, his outrage growing by the second. "From ten million? That's outrageous, Frank. In essence you're handing her a *Get Out of Jail Free* card."

"While I'm grateful for your expert opinion, Mr. Lytell, the ruling stands. Now, if there's nothing else..."

"Chicken shit ruling," Lytell muttered under his breath.

"What's that, Mike?" the judge retorted. "I couldn't quite make you what you said."

"Nothing, Your Honor. It was nothing."

"I certainly hope so." He picked up his gavel and this time slammed it down directly in front of Lytell, who jumped in his seat.

"Dismissed," Hiller said, his angry gaze focused on the D.A. "And don't let the door hit you in the ass on your way out."

Lytell glowered at him but held his tongue. The three of us filed out of the judge's chamber.

Once outside, Lytell exploded, "Fucking travesty of justice."

"Get over it, Mike," Murray Kornbluth said. "You heard Buddy. He fucked up. So what? Cut her some slack."

Lytell looked away.

"You'll draw up the release papers?" Kornbluth asked.

"Sometime today," Lytell responded.

"What's wrong with right now?" I said.

Lytell glared daggers at me "Ah," he said, "the fuck-up speaks."

"You know something, Mike? My father has a saying that's totally appropriate for this occasion."

"Oh, really," Lytell exclaimed. "And what would that saying be?"

"Blow it out your barracks bag."

Chapter Seventeen

Marsha Russo accompanied me as we made our way to the so-called Tombs, the makeshift jail that had been hastily constructed in the basement of the Town Hall building.

"You sure you want to do this?"

"Positive."

"The paperwork hasn't arrived yet."

"Yeah, but it will. I attended the meeting where it was determined. I can see no earthly reason to keep her imprisoned for even one minute longer."

"Even if it looks bad on your record."

I stopped walking and stared at her. "I have no interest in whether this event has an impact on my record. If anyone were to use it as a chance to impugn me or my integrity, then so be it. It's already on my head that she was imprisoned in the first place."

"Actually," Marsha said, "it's on mine."

"Whatever. I challenge anyone to say or do something about it."

"Sir Galahad."

"I'm not kidding around, Marsha."

"I know that, Buddy. I really do. I'm trying to find some light-hearted way of thanking you."

"Not necessary."

"Thank you, just the same."

I smiled as we stepped into the makeshift jail. Kimber was lying on the cot reading when we showed up. She looked at us.

"You might want to think about packing," I said.

"What?"

"You're out, Kimber. Get your stuff."

"You're kidding?"

"He's not," Marsha said.

Kimber stood and began putting her few belongings into the cotton duffel that Marsha handed her. I unlocked the cage and stood aside. Kimber slowly approached. "I don't know what to say. I don't even know how I'll get home."

"Sheriff Steel, here, is planning on driving you," Marsha told her."

She looked at me. "That's not necessary, Buddy. I'll Uber."

I pointed to the duffel. "Is that everything?"

"Yes."

"Let's get out of here."

"I meant it when I said an Uber would be fine."

"I know. My car's parked behind the building. No one will see us leave."

Marsha picked up the duffel. When we reached the rear door, she peered outside. "It's clear."

I hurried to my cruiser and climbed in. Marsha helped Kimber into the passenger side and once she was settled, tapped the roof of the cruiser twice. After making certain she was belted, I fired up the engine and headed out.

Kimber sat silently beside me, watching the landscape slide by as if for the first time. "It changes you."

"Jail?"

"Yes. I wonder if I'll ever see things the same way again."

"Which may be a good thing."

She turned to me. "Why are you doing this?"

"Doing what?"

"Helping me. Getting me fresh clothing. Driving me home."

"This was all my bad."

"How so?"

"You were never warned."

"I should have known."

"Twenty-twenty," I said.

"Hindsight?"

"Yes."

"You still didn't have to do it."

"Is there any chance we could put this behind us?"

She smiled. "You're very sweet."

"What I really am is cynical and cranky."

"You don't fool me, Buddy. I owe you for this."

"How 'bout we call it even?"

"I'll think about it."

I turned into the circular driveway of the small Colonial she had lived in with her husband and pulled to a stop at the front door.

I collected her duffel and helped her out of the cruiser. She unlocked the door and together we went inside. She appeared jittery and uncertain. "Would you mind staying for a few minutes?"

"Spooky?"

"That's not the half of it."

I accompanied her as she walked slowly through each of the rooms, stopping occasionally to examine things. Finally we made it to the kitchen where she pulled out one of the chairs at the small Formica table and sat. She looked around as if in search of something.

"Can I get you anything?"

She focused her gaze on me and nodded. "Whiskey?"

"There's an idea."

I picked up the bottle of Jack Daniel's that stood on the counter beside several other bottles.

"Straight?"

"Definitely."

I poured us each a shot and placed one in front of her. She downed it in a single gulp. She coughed a couple of times. Then she sighed. "This is easily the best-tasting drink I've ever had."

She held out her glass for a refill. This time she took only a sip. "I have no idea what I'm going to do."

"Are you in a rush to decide?"

"No. Not really. I'd certainly like to know why someone killed him. It totally creeped me out. I understand I'll have to start over again, likely somewhere new, but I'm clueless as to where."

She retreated into her thoughts for a while. Her uncertainty was affecting. Her vulnerability made me want to take her in my arms and hold her. Show her that everything was all right. Which would have been a grave error.

She surfaced from her reverie and gazed at me. "I'm okay now, Buddy."

She walked me to the door. "I'm grateful for all you've done for me."

She put her arms around my neck and held tight to me. Her body shook as she briefly sobbed. Then, with her arms still around my neck, she leaned back and stared at me through red-rimmed eyes. Then she let go and pulled back. "I'm sorry. I shouldn't have done that."

Her embrace had taken me by surprise which must have shown on my face.

She quickly opened the door and I stepped outside. I looked back at her.

She smiled briefly and gently closed the door.

I stood rooted to the spot for several moments.

"That was a close call," I mused.

Then I snapped out of it and headed for my cruiser.

Chapter Eighteen

It was a small memorial service held in the Rectory of St. Theresa's Cathedral, officiated by Father Francis Dugan, Freedom's senior cleric—friend and spiritual counselor to any and all who might seek him out. He had been in place for as long as anyone could remember, a wizened man, gentle and kind, short in stature but large in character.

I had first connected with him shortly after my seventeenth birthday, when I was suffering a crisis of faith. My mother had recently passed away after a lengthy battle with ovarian cancer. She had endured a great deal of pain and in the end, she simply surrendered, embraced the opioids she had previously forsworn and soon thereafter, checked out.

For much of her life she had relied on God to guide her along the path. She attended church regularly. She offered herself into the service of her Lord and his daily business. She volunteered readily to work with and support her beloved Father Dugan. But as her strength began to ebb and the illness sapped her spirit, she unwittingly started questioning her faith.

"Why has He forsaken me?" she asked frequently. "What did I do to warrant such suffering?"

Over time she became more and more desolate, wracked with pain and remorse, until ultimately she lost her faith.

She stoically withstood her deterioration with no comfort forthcoming from her Lord. She stopped attending church services. She withdrew from the congregation, unsettled by the realization that her lifelong belief in a Godly heaven had crumbled.

I frequently sat with her, mostly in silence, always aware of her spiritual crisis which, over time, infected me as well.

When she passed, zonked on painkillers, drifting in and out of consciousness, facing the unholy death that was nothing like what she had envisioned, I realized that I, too, had lost my faith.

St. Theresa's Cathedral had been built in the eighteen nineties, in the Gothic-revival style, and its concrete structure had withstood earthquakes, monsoons, and more than its share of ocean-precipitated deterioration. It reeked of incense, dampness, and age.

A small crowd had gathered and the service was about to begin. Marsha Russo and I were in the back, watching the events unfold.

Her Honor, Regina Goodnow, my stepmother and Freedom Township's Mayor was in attendance, as was the school principal, Julia Peterson, along with a number of Freedom High students and faculty.

Kimber Carson sat in the front row, her parents on either side of her. A well-dressed middle-aged couple sat across the aisle, holding hands, clearly grieving. I assumed they were Henry Carson's parents.

Although Father Francis was in excellent form, it was evident he was not an acquaintance of the deceased. He spoke in platitudes and beseeched his Maker to embrace the spirit of Henry Carson and allow him respite from the horrific manner of his passing. He prayed for Carson's eternal peace and salvation. He offered communion and compassion.

I took note of the groupings of the young people in attendance. I recognized Bobby Siegler and Chrissie Lester, the swim team captains. Fred Maxwell, the team coach, was present, along with three of his associates.

Chrissie Lester sat with four young women, all somberly dressed, but withdrawn, not particularly invested in the service. At one point, I noticed two of them engaged with their smartphones. The same held true for several young men, also together, sitting apart from the other attendees, plugged into their devices, uninterested in the service.

Bobby Siegler was near the front, seated with a number of men and women, all raptly tuned into Father Francis. The boys and girls were intermingled in this group. I noticed a few of them holding hands, occasionally gazing at one another. None interacted with their cell phones.

I turned to Marsha and whispered, "Have you noticed the way all of these kids are seated? In those groupings?"

"I have."

"Is there any chance you can find out their names?"

"You mean the kids in each group?"

"Yes."

"I'll give it my best shot."

"Try not to hurt yourself."

She stared at me. "There's something wrong with you, Buddy."

I grinned at her and nodded.

As he neared the conclusion of the service, Father Dugan invited those in attendance to share any thoughts they might have about Coach Carson. No one volunteered. None of the family members chose to speak.

After the Father wrapped things up, the attendees quickly exited the church and scattered. As she and her parents made their exit, Kimber Carson briefly made eye contact with me. Then she was gone.

Father Dugan spotted me and came over. The smile that lit up his face brought a smile to mine, as well. "It's a rare treat seeing you here, Buddy. I wish you'd come around more often."

"It was a lovely service."

"Albeit, an odd one."

"How so?"

"I don't really know. It was strangely devoid of any emotion. Maybe in the intervening days since the murder, they all cried themselves out. But it was likely the driest service I've ever conducted. I pride myself at being able to reach even the most unreachable. I always get at least a few tears. This one was unfathomable."

"Perhaps he wasn't such a likable guy."

"Or maybe I've lost a step or two."

"Who, you?"

"Happens to the best of us."

"Feeling a bit sorry for ourself, are we, Francis?"

"You know me too well, Buddy."

"If it would make you feel any better, had I known the deceased, I surely would have cried."

"Can it, Buddy. I'm not that bad off."

"I'm just saying, is all."

He flashed me his famous dead-eyed stare and changed the subject. "I heard about what happened at Temple Israel."

"The graffiti?"

"I sent a few of my young parishioners over to help Rabbi Weiner clean it up."

"Has me worried."

"Because?"

"This graffiti business is on the verge of becoming a scourge. These idiots have taken to engaging in what they refer to as *metropolitan beautification*, which, translated, means desecrating the landscape. Removing it is costly. And once it's been removed, these taggers are more than likely to target the same spot again."

"I guess we're lucky here at St. Theresa's."

"So far."

"Can you put a stop to it?"

"I'm working on it."

"Let me know if I can help."

"You can pray for them."

"Them who?"

"The taggers."

"Pray for them, why?"

"Because when I catch them, I'm going to make them regret what they've done."

"And you want me to pray for them?"

"I want you to pray for me. Pray that I don't actually kill any of them."

Chapter Nineteen

I arrived at the coffee shop early and was able to score a window table, one that offered a view of Liberty Street Park and the Town Hall across the road.

I was on overload. The investigation into the death of Henry Carson was more complex than I had first imagined. There was a subtext I hadn't yet identified.

The graffiti scourge continued unabated and, unless the penalties were heightened, it would seriously impact the pristine beauty of San Remo County.

I had been on automatic pilot for a spell, but the sudden surge of activity had ratcheted up the stakes. Which presented a genuine challenge. One that carried with it a plethora of anxiety and uncertainty. So much for life in a small town, I thought.

As I sipped my macchiato, I caught sight of Helena Madison loping up the street, graceful as ever, a larger-than-life vision of athleticism in motion.

I watched her enter the shop, collect her coffee, look around, spot me, then head for my table. She put her briefcase on the empty chair beside her and sat facing me.

"Okay," she said. "Come on."

"Come on what?"

"One on one."

"What one on one?"

"You and me, Buddy. Like old times. Just us. One on one. I want to show you what's what one time more."

"What are you, nuts?"

"Possibly. Likely. But be that as it may, I still want one more."

"No."

"You don't want to play because you know I'd whup your ass."

"Possibly. Likely."

"You're just a big chicken, aren't you?"

"Live with it."

She took a swig of coffee. She appeared not a day older than she had when I first met her all those years ago. Her rich chocolate skin was agleam in the sunlight that streamed through the coffee shop window. Thick, wavy hair cascaded chaotically around her face. Her electric eyes were like lasers. Her aquiline nose and ripe red lips completed the portrait. "I have good news and bad. Which do you want first?"

"The bad."

"They turned it down."

"The Town Council?"

"Yes."

"Why?"

"Fear."

"Of?"

"Re-election losses."

"Typical."

"Of?"

"Politicians. You can never trust one."

She chewed on that for a while, concern that I might think less of her darkening her face.

"So, what's the good news?"

"I exercised my prerogatives."

"Is there any chance you might quit speaking in tongues, Helena?"

She leaned across the table and lowered her voice. "I didn't graduate magna cum laude for nothing, you know. Once I got elected to this cockamamie job, I set about studying the rules and by-laws as though they were gospel. And I learned a great deal." She took a sip of coffee and gazed idly at the various tables, momentarily curious as to their occupants and whether or not she knew any of them.

"Go on," I urged.

"In nineteen eighty-seven, an incident occurred in the Town Council that nearly short-circuited the career of the then Council President, guy named Walter Button. This Button character wanted to raise money for some street improvements. Pot holes and stuff. Civic business. But it had become political. Three of the other four members of the Council played for the opposing team and had pledged to vote down Button's proposal."

"So?"

"So he carefully studied the rules and the by-laws and discovered the little-known fact that the accumulation of unclaimed vacation time for Council members could result in a possible double payment, should a Council member request such a payment, as opposed to actually vacationing.

"He further discovered a Town Council addendum that empowered the President to order any member with more than four weeks' worth of accumulated vacation time to immediately take that vacation time. Which resulted in eliminating any possible double payment.

"When President Button learned that each of his three opponents had more than four weeks' worth of unused vacation time, he placed them all on immediate leave and once they were out of the office, he held a vote and his proposition passed unanimously. Two votes to none."

"What is it you're saying here, Helena?"

"As was the case back in Button's day, three members of the current Council have each accumulated more than four weeks' vacation time."

"Which three?"

"I knew you'd ask that question."

"Which three?"

"I may not be ready to disclose that information just yet, Buddy."

"Why?"

"One on one."

"You mean you're not going to finish this story until I agree to go one on one with you?"

"That's right."

"You're an even bigger jerk than I am."

"Taller, too."

She sat silently for a while, her arms smugly folded across her chest.

"Okay. Okay," I said at last.

"Where and when?"

"Your call."

"Your word?"

"You have it."

"Then congratulations."

"What congratulations?"

"I took the vote this morning. Your proposal passed unanimously. Two zip."

"You mean the fines and the jail time are now law?"

"They are."

"For how long?"

"I'm fairly certain that when their vacation time is over and the three bozos return to work, they'll try to vacate the vote.

But I can hold that up for quite some time. My guess would be for at least a year."

"So when I find these taggers, I can make their lives miserable."

"Correct. With but a single caveat."

"One on one."

"Also correct."

"This is very small-minded of you, Helena."

She stared at me for several moments, then began to rub the side of her nose with her extended middle finger.

Chapter Twenty

"I have the names," Marsha Russo said as she plunked herself down in one of my visitor chairs. "I identified them according to the group they sat with at the memorial. I matched them with their yearbook photos."

"And?"

She shoved a copy of the yearbook across the desk. "You might want to have a look at them. The photo pages are all marked with yellow stickies."

I picked up the book and leaned back in my chair. I studied each photo carefully. "There's an odd consistency in the groupings," I commented. "Good-looking versus not-so-good-looking."

"You sure know how to hit the nail on the head, big boy. The mixed group, boys and girls, they're all very attractive. The other groups, not so much."

"Which you interpret as?"

"I don't know, Buddy. If what Kimber suspected regarding the possibility of sexual shenanigans is true, the fact that there was this grouping of only good-looking kids sitting together at the memorial might have some bearing."

"It might."

"It's certainly worthy of further investigation."

"It certainly is."

Marsha sat back in her chair, more than a little self-satisfied with her findings. "Would you want to interview any of these kids?"

"I would."

"Which ones?"

"Let's start with the questionably unattractive ones."

"That's an unfortunate nomenclature."

"Okay. How about the not-so-good-looking ones."

"Too subjective."

"Then how about separating them by sex? Boys and girls."

"Bingo," she said and stood. "I'll start organizing the list."

"This is very good work, Marsha."

"I thought so." She sauntered out of my office.

●●●●●

Peter Bry agreed to meet me in Longdale, a couple of towns over from Freedom, in a small, family-owned sandwich shop where it was unlikely we would be spotted.

I arrived before he did and from a table in the rear, I watched as the muscular young man stepped tentatively up to the shop window and scanned the place. When he noticed I was there, he came inside and joined me.

"Thank you for seeing me, Peter."

He nodded.

"Coffee?"

"Maybe an energy drink."

I signaled the waitress who took the order, then wandered off to fill it. Bry turned to me. "This is about the murder, right?"

"Yes."

"Horrible tragedy."

"It was, yes."

"I don't really know anything about it."

"I didn't expect you would."

"But you wanted to speak with me just the same?"

"I did."

"Why?"

The waitress delivered his order then scurried off.

I watched Peter Bry as he opened and then poured his can of electrolyte-packed liquid into a plastic cup. He gulped some of it down. He was a strapping young man, fit but unfortunately burdened with a nose the size of a small country and ears almost equally as large. He was bright-eyed, however, and quick-witted. He was engaging and engaged.

"I'm trying to learn as much as I can about Henry Carson is why. Since you're the swim team workhorse, or so that's what I've been told, I thought you might have some insights that could be helpful."

"Such as?"

"Well, for openers, did you like him?"

He reached for his right ear and scooped out a piece of shmutz which he stared at for a moment before whisking it away. "I never really thought about that before. Did I like him? No. Actually, I didn't like him at all."

"Why not?"

Bry shifted uneasily in his chair, seemingly nervous to be speaking so frankly. "He was a weird guy. He paid lots of attention to the good-looking kids. A few of the boys. All of the girls. He would nod and say hello to me. He wasn't rude or anything. But he pretty much ignored me."

"And the other coaches?"

"Coach Fred is great. So are the others. They evaluate my performances and offer suggestions as to how I can improve them. They're involved in the details and are amazingly helpful and encouraging."

"But not Coach Hank."

"Not Coach Hank."

"And that's why you didn't like him?"

"I didn't like him because he never invited me to any of the play parties."

"The play parties?"

The young man vanished into his thoughts for a moment, then stared at me and said, "Look, I don't think I want to go into this stuff. I don't really have a whole lot of information about it."

"What's a play party?"

"I don't know. I never went to one. I only heard rumors."

"What kind of rumors?"

"That there was fooling around."

"What kind of fooling around?"

"Like I said, I only heard rumors. You should ask some of the girls."

"How often did these play parties take place?"

"Look, I already told you I don't really know anything about them. Only the bits and pieces I overheard."

"Like there was fooling around going on."

Bry leaned forward and planted his elbows on the table. "This is making me real uncomfortable. I'm sorry I ever said anything. All I know is that there were play parties. Parties to which me and most of the other team members weren't invited. That's all I know."

"Parties where there was fooling around, as you termed it. I'm presuming fooling around refers to some kind of sexual activity."

Peter Bry pushed back his chair and stood.

"I never said that. I told you all I know. I could get in trouble for this."

He looked around the sandwich shop as if to make certain he hadn't been noticed or overheard. "I gotta go now."

He looked at me for a couple of moments, then made tracks for the door.

I watched him go. I paid the tab and headed for my car. "Play parties," I muttered to myself. "What in the hell is a play party?"

Chapter Twenty-one

"A play party is one that encourages sexual or polyamorous activities," Marsha Russo read to me from a blog she had discovered on the Internet.

"Define polyamorous."

"Non-monogamous. The play party phenomenon appears to have begun in the East. And it's not just restricted to normal sexual behavior, it's also big in the BDSM community."

"BDSM?"

"A composite acronym. B for bondage, DS for dominance and submission, and SM for sado-masochism."

"Who goes to these parties?"

"They seem to cut a wide swath. At least according to what I read on the Internet. Swingers. Group sex aficionados. Recreational sex advocates. People who experiment with their sexual expression."

"Where do I sign up?"

"You know something, Buddy? I wish you were half as funny as you think you are."

I flashed her my goofiest smile.

"Shall we get on with this or do you want to just roll around in your adolescent mire?"

"Adolescent?"

"Is it at all possible for you to treat this subject with at least a small measure of maturity?"

"Who, me?"

She glared at me. We were in her tiny cubicle, she in front of an Apple desktop, me seated behind her, trying to look over her shoulder but not really able to make out the small print showing on the screen. "So, how does it work?" I prodded.

"Well, there's no saying how it worked with Hank Carson and the swim team, but generally speaking, the Internet explains that a play party is an invitation-only event, involving numbers of people and multiple partners. Nudity is almost always involved. Permission to play is a must. Proper hygiene and safe sex are *de rigueur*. Participation is voluntary and involves all kinds of sexual activity. Those invitees who would prefer to simply watch from the sidelines are encouraged to do so, as long as they don't interfere with the actual players. No unwelcome touching of a player is permitted, but masturbation is encouraged. What else do you want to know?"

"How widespread is it?"

"You mean the play party phenomenon?"

"Yes."

"It's worldwide."

"How do you know?"

"It's all over the 'Net."

"You mean people have these kind of parties everywhere?"

"Young and old. Straight and gay. Dominant and submissive. Everywhere."

"I find it hard to believe."

"Well, you better start believing, Mr. Smarty Pants Deputy Sheriff, because it looks like it's going on right here in Freedom High School, of all places. Directly under your ignorant nose."

Chapter Twenty-two

"Two more this morning," Johnny Kennerly said.

He was in his cruiser on a cell phone. I was in my office.

"I'm sorry," I said, trying to snap myself out of the deepening darkness in which the play party phenomenon was threatening to engulf me. "What did you say?"

"Fielbert's Garden Supplies and Rogie's Donair Emporium. Every available inch of their wall space has been spray-painted with weird drawings and oversized letters. All of them signed, I might add."

"Robber Xmas?"

"Mostly, yes."

"I think we've reached critical mass. It's time to raise the stakes."

"How do we do that?"

"By getting the word out that we're serious about apprehending these dickheads. Big rewards for those who lead us to them. Big penalties once they're caught."

"And we go about doing this how?"

"We print Wanted signs and post them everywhere. Every possible Internet outlet should be posted as well. We establish a Graffiti Hot Line and man it twenty-four/seven."

"How do you propose we pay for all this?"

"By legislative decree. Which has already been granted."

"You mean the Council is going to fund this?"

"I do."

"How did you arrange that?"

"Helena Madison."

"No shit. Helena's gotten this approved?"

"She has."

"No shit," Johnny repeated. "How did you get her to do it?"

"I said yes to a little one on one contest."

"Excuse me?"

"She and I are going to play a little one on one together."

"What are you, crazy? She'll wipe the floor with you."

"Is there any way I might convince you to keep your opinions to yourself?"

Johnny snickered. "Oh, baby. This, I can't wait to see."

• • ● • •

"Play parties," my father exclaimed.

We were having lunch on the back patio of his house, his favorite spot, more so because it had also been cherished by my late mother.

It was a balmy, windswept afternoon and a pair of red-topped house finches caught my attention as they chased each other around the yard, stopping on occasion to forage for something to eat, then noisily resuming the chase.

Lunch for me was a chicken salad sandwich. The Sheriff's was a peanut butter and jelly, which was all he was currently able to eat. His health was still on a downward spiral and he had begun to experience difficulty swallowing. Rather than adopting a liquid diet, he became defiant, forcing himself to eat solids, and having some success with the PB and J. "So, that's what was going on?"

"Seems to be all the rage. Marsha read me blog postings from play party participants all over the world. Without going into detail, it does appear that this phenomenon has caught on big-time. Reflective, I'm guessing, of the changing philosophy regarding sex and commitment."

"Changing how?"

"A loosening of moral standards, perhaps. The rejection of traditional values such as marriage and monogamy as the sole criteria for sexual relationships."

"Must be right up your alley."

This comment hit home. "What's that supposed to mean?"

"Sounds like your kind of lifestyle."

"Where are you going with this, Burton?"

"You're what now, thirty-four?"

"Thirty-two."

He looked more closely at me, as if he were appraising my candidacy for non-monogamous hook-ups. "Whatever," he muttered. "You never married. Never even had a girl you thought seriously enough about to bring home. Aren't you a perfect example of a changing world philosophy regarding sex and commitment?"

"I'm not sure I would agree with that. You don't see me involved in any play parties."

"Probably because you didn't know they existed."

It struck me that the old man was purposely needling me. I discovered the edges of a smile at the corners of his mouth. And even though I was his victim, it pleased me to see him rising to the occasion. "Were you looking to get my goat this morning?"

"Hey, if the shoe fits."

"It doesn't fit. Okay?"

I pushed my plate back and stood.

"Oh, sit down, Buddy. Don't be so thin-skinned. I'm the one who's dying here, remember?"

I sat back down, somewhat contrite. I took a bite of my sandwich and with my mouth still full, offered, "This play party thing might conceivably have had some connection to Henry Carson's death."

"Because?"

"There's a rift happening between members of the swim team."

"Where he was a coach."

"Less a coach than a kind of glorified consultant—whose attentions were directed not toward the team as a whole, but only to certain members of the team."

"What certain members?"

"The better-looking ones. There's an undercurrent of resentment among the kids who didn't make the cut."

"You mean the not-so-good-looking ones."

"So it would appear."

"Proof?"

"Not yet. I first heard the term *play party* from one of the swim team kids who hadn't been invited to any of them. He said he had no actual knowledge of what took place at one, but whatever went on was ultra hush hush. Then he became frightened and ended our interview."

"So, what's next?"

"Further investigation."

"This could get nasty."

"I think it already is. Someone killed Hank Carson. Someone who knew him. Someone who was likely wounded by him. I'm going to find that person."

We both sat silently. I finished my sandwich and watched as my father wrestled with his. He took tiny bites and chewed carefully. He was earnest about it and it was difficult to watch. At some point, he put the sandwich down and sat back in his chair. "You also mentioned something about graffiti."

"Have you seen it?"

"No."

"Are you up for a little ride?"

"With you?"

"Why not?"

"I wish I thought more highly of your driving."

"Ditto," I said.

We toured Freedom and the neighboring townships. I showed him the places that I knew had been defaced. And we discovered a couple of new ones along the way. He shook his head. "Why would anyone do such a thing?"

"The prevailing wisdom in the universe of the graffiti artist seems to be, '*If I want to paint something, I'll damn well do it. Anywhere I choose. Public property, private property. It's all the same to me.*'"

"Talk about disrespect."

"There have been half-hearted attempts to stop them, but although the defacement of both public and private property is clearly an act of vandalism, these self-righteous, sanctimonious assholes somehow manage to get away with it."

"How do they do that?"

"They regard themselves as groundbreakers of a new art form. Street art. The wave of the future. Surpassing modern art, postmodern art, and contemporary art.

"They believe an empty wall belongs to whomever sees it first, regardless of whose property it might be on. They think of themselves as superstars. They even sign their so-called work.

"The worst of it is that this tagging, as it's called, has become a worldwide scourge. It's everywhere. Removing it is no longer possible because as soon as they clean up one piece of graffiti, it's soon replaced by another. As a result, more and more cities are rife with this crap and local governments seem no longer able to combat it."

"Because?"

"It costs a fortune to remove. And even if they spent that fortune, it would be to no avail. These rats live in the shadows. They perform their defacements in the dead of night. They're like stealth bombers who travel around freely, never identifying themselves beyond their signature tags. Cops can't identify them, never mind apprehend them.

"And not only that, if anyone did find them, the penalties for what they've done are meaningless. Not even the equivalent of a slap on the wrist."

"So what can we do about it?"

"You mean here in Freedom?"

"Yes."

"We find them and take them down."

"If no one else can find them, how can you?"

I pulled into the driveway and parked in front of the Sheriff's house. I turned off the engine and lowered the windows. We stayed seated in the car.

"The Town Council has agreed to heighten the penalties. Large fines and jail time."

"How did you convince them to do that?"

"Helena Madison. She gets it."

The Sheriff chortled. "I still don't see how you can find any of these clowns when no one else can."

"Because I'm obsessed. I'll find them, all right, and when I do, I'm going to make their lives miserable."

"Good luck with that, Buddy."

"That's what everyone says."

Chapter Twenty-three

"The widow on line five," Wilma Hansen announced.

"The widow?"

"Yeah. You know. The runner. Kimber Carson. Would you like me to monitor the call?"

"That won't be necessary.'"

"She's a suspect, right?"

"That's questionable."

"What if she were to say something incriminating?"

"That's not likely, Wilma."

She soldiered on, her intention being to rile me, an ongoing effort which never failed to please her. She was a handsome woman in her late thirties, and if she weren't happily married, I'd think she had a crush on me. Maybe she does have a crush on me. Who knows? But I nonetheless enjoy her jibes. Even when they're at my expense. Taking shots at the boss works wonders for morale. And every so often, they're hilarious.

"But what if she did say something incriminating? Be better to have another pair of ears on the line."

"Thanks, but no thanks."

"You could live to regret this decision, Buddy."

"I'll take my chances."

"Okay. It's your call. But when push comes to shove, don't say I didn't offer," she said and clicked off.

"Kimber?"

"Buddy?"

"Yes."

"Is this out of line?"

"Is what out of line?"

"My calling you like this."

"Not at all."

"Would my asking you to dinner be out of line?"

"Are you asking me to dinner?"

"Yes. A home-cooked dinner."

"You want to cook dinner for me?"

"Are you always this obtuse?"

"Obtuse?"

"Listen, Buddy. I'm inviting you to dinner. At my house. I'm prepared to whip up my world-class pot roast along with roasted potatoes and mixed veggies. I thought it would be better if we met in private. Nobody around to spy on us."

"You're really serious about this?"

"Totally."

"Okay. When?"

"Tonight?"

"Okay."

"Drinks at seven."

"Okay."

"Dinner to follow."

"Okay."

"Stop saying that."

"Okay. What can I bring?"

"Your appetite. Seven o'clock." She ended the call.

After I placed the receiver onto its cradle, I leaned back in my chair and quietly chastised myself. "Buddy," I muttered, "you may be nuttier than a fruitcake."

Chapter Twenty-four

I left the cruiser at home and drove my own car, an ancient Jeep Wrangler, and parked it a couple of blocks from her house. It wouldn't do for the Deputy Sheriff's car to be seen in front of it.

I hoofed it to the house and she had the door open before I even rang the bell. "I was watching for you."

I handed her the bottle of Argentinian Malbec I had brought. She smiled and led me inside.

An air of uncertainty permeated the small bungalow. The residue of death lingered in the unsettled atmosphere. Kimber seemed freighted with insecurity, a person who had been unexpectedly derailed and forced to reconsider her premises. Alone with me, she seemed uncertain as to how she should behave.

I took the Malbec from her and opened it. I poured her a glass and when I handed it to her, she immediately took a large gulp before I poured my own glass and had the chance to toast her.

"Oops," she said, realizing her mistake.

She smiled sheepishly and raised her glass to me.

"To better times," I toasted.

She led me to the living room's twin upholstered armchairs and motioned for me to sit across from her. The room was sparsely furnished, devoid of any noticeable attempts at interior design. No paintings hung on the walls. Very few books were on the bookcase. I spied no photos of her and her late husband. A three-seater sofa was in front of a wall-mounted, fifty-two-inch Samsung wide-screen TV, along with a low-lying coffee table and a pair of side tables.

She watched me as I took note of the surroundings. She seemed tired, although in her pale blue sheath, with her streaked hair askew, and her large hazel eyes ablaze, she was a genuine temptation. She shrugged. "Maybe this wasn't such a good idea."

"I'm glad you suggested it."

"You are?"

"For what it's worth, I believe you were blindsided by what happened to your husband. Forced to adopt an entirely different set of life protocols. Not at all easy. I'm impressed at how well you're handling it."

"You are?"

I nodded.

"How could you, of all people, say such a thing? I skipped town. You had to come arrest me. I must be a colossal pain in the ass for you."

"Not true. Besides, it's my fault you left in the first place."

She drank a large swallow of wine, more intent on quantity than quality. "I'm lost, Buddy," she blurted. "I have no friends. No real job anymore. I mean, who would buy a house from me now? Nobody even takes my call. I'm a pariah. And I'm stuck in this house with the ghost of my dead husband haunting me. And what's worse is I'll have to stay until his murder is solved and I'm no longer a suspect. I'm totally pathetic."

She shielded her face from me when the tears began to fall. "You're the only person I can talk to. The only person who's been kind to me."

I stood and pulled her to her feet. I took her in my arms and held her. She wept.

After a while the sobs subsided and she stopped trembling. She stepped back sought out my eyes. "Can you forgive me?"

"Nothing to forgive."

She looked away and gulped down another swallow of wine. "Are you hungry?" she asked, tentatively.

"Famished."

She managed a smile. "Then you've come to the right place." She took my hand and led me into the kitchen.

● ● ● ● ●

We pushed back the chairs, having eaten our fill. She hadn't been kidding when she referred to it as world-class pot roast. I can't remember having eaten better.

I helped her clear the table and then she waved me off as she set about loading the dishwasher. "There's brandy," she said. "Why don't you pour us a couple while I finish up in here?"

"Sounds like a plan."

I wandered into the living room where I found a bottle of Hennessy and a pair of snifters. I happily tested its scent and then poured us each a healthy serving. I placed Kimber's on the table next to her chair. I grabbed mine and sat. The brandy took immediate hold of me and my thoughts began to drift.

Primarily I was concerned with what exactly I was doing in this house with this woman. She was a key figure in a murder investigation I was conducting, and as such, was taboo. But when she entered the living room, wearing the low-cut, pale blue sheath dress that inadvertently called attention to her every curve, my breath caught.

She picked up her glass and raised it in my direction. "Again to better times." We both drank. Then she sat with her legs curled beneath her. "What should we talk about?"

"Have you ever heard of play parties?"

She sat quietly for a few moments. "Why do you ask?"

"One of the swim team boys mentioned there were play parties at Freedom High. Well, not exactly at Freedom High, but connected to it."

"He mentioned them in relation to my husband?"

"I think so."

"You think so?"

"I was interviewing him about the murder when he brought them up."

"So it was in relation to Henry?"

"Perhaps indirectly. Did your husband ever mention play parties to you?"

She took another sip of brandy. "My husband pretty much stopped talking to me after we moved to Freedom."

"Why?"

"I wish I knew. Prior to Freedom, when we were still in New Jersey, we talked endlessly. We made love frequently. We were close. But when we moved here, he became distant, obsessed with his work. Uncommunicative. And we stopped having sex.

"When I tried to discuss it with him, it made him angry. He withdrew even further. When I suggested family therapy, he laughed me off."

"What did you do?"

"I went on a hunt for a proper psychiatrist and began seeing her regularly. Twice a week."

"And?"

"I realized how emotionally wounded I was. How little I understood myself. So I went on a mission."

"A mission?"

"My shrink told me that learning about myself was as important as any other kind of education. I set out to learn as much as I could about me. About how best to handle the situation I was confronting. To stop seeking ways to ameliorate the circumstance and focus instead on how best to handle my own emotions. In time I came to realize I couldn't be with a man who no longer wanted to be with me. I asked him for a divorce."

"Did anyone know that?"

"My parents. We discussed my moving back home for a while. Until I could regain my footing. They agreed it was a good idea."

"And?"

"Somebody killed him."

"Have you any thoughts about who it was or why?"

"None. We were living in separate worlds. Aside from briefly meeting the Principal, Julia Peterson, I had no dealings with any of his associates."

She finished her brandy and she held out the glass for more. I poured. She briefly sniffed, then sipped. "This stuff goes straight to my head."

Her eyes had developed a slight glaze, a softening of sharpness, a faint absence of focus. Noticing this, I commented, "I think I should be leaving."

"Would I be out of line if I asked you to stay?"

A brief glimpse of sensuality flashed in her eyes, a look filled with promise and expectation. She took another sip of brandy, stood somewhat unsteadily and whispered, "Don't leave."

I scrambled to my feet. "I can't stay with you, Kimber. You're very desirable. More than you know. But it would be a mistake. For both of us."

I shook my head and made for the door. She took a few steps as if to follow.

I turned back to her. "Thank you for the wonderful dinner."

I let myself out.

Once in the Wrangler, I turned on the engine and sat back

in the driver's seat. I commended myself on having avoided what I innately knew was a pathway to heartache.

But it was a close call. In different times I would have stayed. I'd have thought I could change things for her. Ease her pain. Make things better.

But she wore her hurt like a badge and although she was surely tempting, the choice to be with her was exactly the type of psychological misstep I had made in the past.

I took a deep breath.

Instead of having leapt into an emotional abyss, I had actually made the healthy choice. And although once I got home I would be alone, it was an alone I could handle.

"Maybe there's hope for me yet," I chided myself.

Chapter Twenty-five

The banner headline on the police flier screamed:

WANTED: GRAFFITI ARTIST KNOWN AS ROBBER XMAS
REWARD FOR INFORMATION LEADING TO HIS ARREST

Three photos of his spray-painted graffiti appeared on the flier, which had been posted and e-mailed throughout the state. The fliers were impossible to miss. They were everywhere.

Johnny Kennerly burst into my office. "Listen to this," he said excitedly. "Once the fliers hit L.A., I got this call from the LAPD liaison in charge of the graffiti task force there. Guy called Chuck Voight."

"I know Chuck Voight. We were rookies together."

"That's what he said. He also said he had some great Buddy Steel stories."

I knew Chuck Voight to be an inveterate kibbitzer who'd stop at nothing to get a laugh.

"Pay no attention to his stories, okay? He makes stuff up."

"That's what he told me you'd say."

"He pioneered the 'alternative facts' phenomenon."

"He mentioned you'd say that too. In any event, this Voight guy knows about Robber Xmas. L.A. cops have been trying to locate him since the Mayor got serious about putting an end to the graffiti scourge."

"And?"

"No luck. But they're still searching. And he claims LAPD will do whatever it can to help find him. Says he wants to talk with you about how we can interface. Particularly since Mr. Xmas is operating in both of our territories."

"I'll call him."

"My talk with him gave me an idea," Johnny said.

"Okay."

"This Robber Xmas guy. He showed up in Freedom out of the blue. Just after Labor Day. And he's been tagging here ever since."

"So what's the idea?"

"He's got to live somewhere. I want to canvas the town in search of new arrivals. Rentals. Resident hotels. New home sales. Boardinghouses. It's probably a shot in the dark, but you never know."

"Go for it."

"You think?"

"Why not? It's as good as anything we're doing now."

"I'll let Detective Voight know."

"Good idea."

"And maybe he'll even tell me a story or two."

"Lies. All lies. Don't waste your time."

"It'll be the best time I ever wasted. I can hardly wait."

"He's an idiot," I said and shooed Johnny out of my office.

Chapter Twenty-six

Steffi Lincoln's assignment was to swim the third leg of the two-mile relay. She was a sturdy young woman, barrel-chested with muscular arms and large, powerful legs. She wasn't a great beauty, but she was smart and funny, a consummate swimmer and a team favorite.

"I don't know anything about that," she stated in answer to my question about play parties.

"Surely you knew they were taking place."

She had reluctantly agreed to speak with me, but only in the presence of her mother, Selma, a stern-looking woman in her late forties who leveled a flinty glare at me.

We were sitting in the deserted stands of the pool house. It was five o'clock, practice was finished for the day and Coach Maxwell had given us the green-light to meet there.

"You read lips?" Steffi asked me.

"I don't."

"Well, try to read mine anyway. I don't know anything about play parties. Period."

"So you were never invited to one."

She turned to her mother. "I told you this was a bad idea."

"Try to be a little more cooperative, honey," Selma Lincoln said. "One of your coaches was murdered. Try to keep that in mind."

"You don't have to be so cynical, Mother."

She looked back at me. "Was there anything else?"

I liked Steffi Lincoln. She had character and she unabash-edly spoke her mind. She seemed comfortable in her skin and self-confidence was the cornerstone of her persona. If she had emotional misgivings about Henry Carson and his behavior with the other swim team girls, she didn't reveal them.

"Was Mr. Carson involved with these parties?"

"As far as I could see, he was pretty much involved with everything. But I wouldn't know specifically about any parties."

"What did you mean about him being pretty much involved with everything?"

"I don't know. I must have misspoken."

"Why is this so difficult?" I muttered.

She scowled at me.

"Okay, let me start over. Why did you say he was *pretty much involved with everything*?"

She shrugged. "Look," she began, "my vantage point was from the outside looking in. My knowledge of him was from that perspective. I don't really know what he did or didn't do. He was much more interested in the other girls than he was in me."

"Why?"

"Isn't it obvious?"

"Not to me."

"Look at me. I look like some kind of overdeveloped slug. He was only interested in the pretty ones."

"Why, do you suppose?"

"I thought he was some kind of lech. He was always hanging around, always leering. Freaky like. I heard he even tried to get into some of the girls' pants."

"How do you know that?"

"I think this line of questioning is off point," Selma Lincoln interjected.

I looked at her. "It's very much on point. I'm trying to learn whether Mr. Carson was directly involved with play parties."

"Steffi has already told you she knows nothing about them."

"But she did say Mr. Carson was some kind of lech."

"No. She said she thought he might be a lech."

"Who was trying to get into some of the girls' pants."

"Look," Selma Lincoln said, "Steffi made no specific allegations and she repeatedly said she knew nothing about these play parties you keep referencing."

She stood and motioned to her daughter. "I think we're done here."

"I have just a few more questions."

"Not even one," she said. "Good day, Sheriff Steel."

I got up and looked at Steffi for a few moments. She also stood and made eye contact.

I took out one of my business cards and handed it to her. "In case you think of something you might have overlooked."

"Thank you."

She put the card in her pocket and the two of them left the pool house.

Curious and curiouser, I thought. This child knows more than she's letting on. She's afraid of something. Afraid of saying something that might reveal more than what she believes she's permitted to reveal.

I wondered what that was all about.

Chapter Twenty-seven

The drive from Freedom to Los Angeles took less than two hours. I avoided rush hour and because I was in a police cruiser, the traffic tended to get out of my way. I pulled into the Musso & Frank parking lot just before one o'clock.

Located in the center of Hollywood, down the street from such landmarks as Grauman's Chinese, The Hollywood Wax Museum, and the El Capitan Theatre, Musso's is a legendary industry eatery. Its grill room was where Charlie Chaplin lunched daily in his exclusive corner booth which, in later years, was where Steve McQueen, Nelson Riddle, and Jonathan Winters could be regularly found. It's still the favorite of movie and TV luminaries who frequent the area.

Because it was a place neither of us could afford when we were rookie cops together, Chuck Voight chose it for our lunch. He even reserved the Chaplin booth.

He was already seated when I arrived and he stood to greet me. After a hail of compliments regarding our respective appearances and a good deal of mutual back-slapping and laughter, we slid into the red leather, dark mahogany wood booth that faced Hollywood Boulevard, both of us with big grins on our faces.

"One time, when I made Detective, Daryl Gates brought

me here," Voight reminisced. "He so scared the shit out of me that I ordered scrambled eggs thinking nothing else would stay down."

"Why don't you have the eggs today?" I taunted him. "For old times' sake."

"Screw that, Buddy boy. Steak. Medium rare. Mashed garlic potatoes. Us guys have arrived."

"Martinis?"

"I'm on duty."

"Never stopped you before."

"Yeah, well, we've come a long way since them days. Back then I could handle it. Today I'd go face-first into the mashed."

His imagery made me laugh. "You're not alone, Charley. It's great to see you."

"You, too. You enjoying yourself up there in Shitsville?"

"Not totally."

"Something about your father, right?"

"Lou Gehrig's disease."

"Oh, Jeez. I'm sorry, Buddy."

"Thanks."

"People miss you down here. I can't tell you how many times guys ask me how you're doing."

"That's nice. Thanks for mentioning it."

"My pleasure. I always tell them you're in a rehab facility in Malibu."

I snorted.

A smartly dressed waiter in a red tuxedo jacket stepped to our booth brandishing a platter of sourdough bread along with his best wise-guy attitude. "How did you two suckers manage to score the Chaplin?"

"Pull," Voight said.

"Cops," the waiter said. "I could spot you a mile away."

"That obvious, huh?"

"Like you've got name tags on your foreheads. What can I get you?"

We told him. He grinned and strolled off.

I watched him go, then asked, "Robber Xmas?"

"If it's the last thing I do."

"He's that slippery?"

Voight shook his head. "Son of a bitch is on my radar. I keep thinking I'm warm, but I can't quite close the deal. Your associate tells me he's shifted operations to your neck of the woods."

"Could be. How often do you monitor your landscape?"

"For graffiti, you mean?"

"Yes."

"Regularly. Daily."

"When was the last time you saw something of his?"

"Nothing new for a couple of weeks now."

"How long had he been tagging here?"

"At least a year. Maybe more."

"And you haven't been able to identify him?"

"He works alone. Sometimes we don't see anything from him for several weeks. Then he re-surfaces with a flurry. Unpredictable."

The waiter arrived with our steaks, fresh from the grill, sensationally aromatic. A similarly clad staffer brought Chuck's mashed and my baked. Plus the side order of creamed spinach we were sharing. The waiter handed us each a steak knife. "Management frowns on ripping the meat off the bone with your teeth."

He laughed at his joke and left us to our feast.

"How can we help each other?" I asked after we had dug in.

"We need to track his patterns. I'll let you know if he shows up back here. Or if I learn anything in his absence. You do the same."

"A regular joint task force," I offered.

"I don't know about that," Chuck added. "This guy's a slippery son of a bitch. But at least we'll get the chance to make some more mischief together. Like that time in Boyle Heights."

"Don't go there, Chuck."

"Oh, come on, Buddy. Surely you remember that night."

"If I did, which I don't, it would be a totally different memory than the one you have."

"That's a load of crap. You haven't forgotten the milk shake incident, have you?"

"There was no milk shake incident. You made it up."

"All six of them?"

"Four."

"Four what?"

"Four of them."

"So it is true."

"Maybe some of it is true."

"You're so full of shit, Buddy. Remember how sick you got?"

"No, I don't remember getting sick at all."

"Liar."

"Liar yourself. Eat your steak before it gets cold." He punched my arm playfully.

"Ditto."

We laughed our way through the rest of the meal.

Chapter Twenty-eight

"I may have something," Johnny Kennerly said. "A bungalow in South Freedom. Sold in late August. To a real estate trust. Paid for in cash."

I was in my cruiser, heading back to the station. "What about it?"

"It's an anomaly."

"Meaning?"

"I don't know, Buddy. Low-rent part of town like that. Unexceptional house sells to a trust for cash. It's not your typical investment property. Something about it doesn't smell kosher."

"What's the address?"

He told me.

"I'm not too far from there. I'll give it the once-over and let you know," I said and ended the call.

It was a short drive to 321 Meeker Street and I slowed when I got there. The house in question was a single-story bungalow, one of six tract houses, but unlike its neighbors, it appeared unattended, in need of maintenance. It hadn't been painted in some time. The windows were streaked with grime. A small yard was overgrown with wildflowers and weeds. It was out of character for the neighborhood.

I drove past it and saw that the other houses in the tract were respectfully tended, yards were trimmed, and late model cars stood in several of the driveways.

I pulled up in front of the house next door and got out of my cruiser. I wanted to take a closer look at number 321. As I began nosing around, a frazzled house-frau who appeared to be in her thirties stepped outside and stared at me with a puzzled look on her face.

"Nobody's there," she called out.

She wore a stained apron over a faded housedress that at one time might have been blue. Her pale auburn hair was highlighted with streaks of purple. She wore thick-rimmed glasses. She was barefoot.

She looked at my cruiser, then shifted her gaze onto me. "You're a cop, right?"

"Deputy Sheriff," I said. "Buddy Steel."

"Is there some kind of trouble?"

"Not at all. I'm sorry to bother you, but I noticed the house looks as if it might be deserted. I was wondering if you could tell me whether or not people actually live there."

"Why?" the woman asked.

"In the interest of public safety. We regularly check neighborhoods for unoccupied houses. Houses that could become havens for drugs and crime."

The woman nodded. "Judy Nicholas."

"Excuse me?"

"I'm Judy Nicholas. Nick's wife."

"Mrs. Nicholas," I said.

"Somebody does live in that house. Some sleazeball who takes lousy care of it and who's single-handedly responsible for lowering the value of the other houses on the block."

"I take it you're unhappy with the owner."

"The son of a bitch bought the house for a song. It hadn't

been lived in since the original owner killed himself over a year ago. Nobody wanted to buy it what with the suicide and all. Guy shot himself. A bloody mess. So we were pretty excited when it finally sold. But the bastard hasn't done one thing to improve it."

"But he lives in it?"

"Sometimes he does. Sometimes he doesn't. He comes and goes."

"When did you last see him?"

"Maybe a week ago."

"What does he do?"

"I wouldn't know. Nothing, probably."

A small boy appeared in the doorway. Still in his pajamas, he walked over and stood beside Mrs. Nicholas. He grabbed hold of her apron and stuck his thumb in his mouth. He wasn't exactly the cleanest little kid I'd ever seen, but he was alert and engaged. He didn't say anything but he didn't miss anything either.

I nodded to him.

He took a step backward and inched closer to his mother who, in turn, ignored him. "Was there anything else you wanted to know?"

"Would you by any chance know the name of the owner?"

"Only his first name."

"Which is?"

"Robert."

"Robert. Thank you, Mrs. Nicholas. You've been very helpful."

I handed her one of my cards. "Perhaps you could phone me when the owner returns."

"I will. Maybe you could scare the bastard into improving his property."

I smiled at her and headed for my cruiser.

I heard the little boy shout, "Hey. Mister."

I turned back to him.

He raised his hand and pointed to himself. "I'm Nick, Junior," he said.

"Pleased to meet you, Nick, Junior. I'm Buddy, Junior."

"Really?"

"Yep."

He grinned at me, looked up at his mother and then ran inside.

"The previous owner was a guy called Leonard Sherman," Johnny Kennerly read aloud. "Born: May 5, 1955. Died: May 5, 2015."

"Born and died on the same day," I commented. "What are the odds of that?"

"Pretty good, considering he shot himself."

"Oh, yeah. Mrs. Nicholas did mention something about that."

We were in Johnny's cubicle and he was in front of his laptop, on some kind of real estate website. "House was on the market for nearly a year until it was sold to the G.V.N. Real Estate Trust for considerably less than it had come on the market for."

"What's the G.V.N. Real Estate Trust?"

"Good question. Seems it's managed by a Beverly Hills law firm."

"Beverly Hills?"

"Strange, isn't it?"

"Have you been in touch with them?"

"Not yet. I wanted your advice as to how best to go about it."

"Maybe when the owner returns, we might do a little sur-veilling before we tip our hand."

"Meaning?"

"Let's see who lives there and what it is he goes about doing."

"Do we tell Chuck Voigt?"

"Not until we know more."

"I guess that's a plan."

I nodded. "That'd be my guess, too."

Chapter Twenty-nine

It seemed as if I had just fallen asleep when my cell phone began ringing. When I looked, it was past nine. I overslept.

"Buddy Steel," I answered sleepily.

"Bad news," Marsha Russo said.

I immediately thought the worst about my father before she went on to say, "Steffi Lincoln."

"What about her?"

"She was badly beaten on her way to school this morning."

"By whom?" I said, sitting up in bed.

"Don't know. She arrived at Freedom General about fifteen minutes ago and she's still being evaluated."

"I'm on my way."

"Me, too," Marsha said.

• • ● • •

The Emergency Room was jumping when I arrived at ten-thirty. The waiting room was full, as was the trauma center.

I was greeted by Head Nurse Jill MacDonough, whom I'd known since high school. Small town. She ushered me to the ICU where Steffi Lincoln was being treated.

"What should I know?" I asked.

"Well, for openers, it's not life-threatening," Jill said. "She was pretty upset when she got here and Amir put her on a sedative drip. Contusions and bruising. She'll need a few stitches and that shiner will linger for a few days, but otherwise she'll be okay."

We stepped inside.

Dr. Amir Abboud was dealing with a rather mean-looking head wound. He looked at me and nodded.

Steffi's mother, Selma, sat in the corner. When she saw me, she glowered, the look in her eyes ranging from angry to downright hostile. I motioned for her to step outside.

Once in the hall, she unloaded. "This is because you insisted on interviewing her. Without that, it would never have happened."

I saw Marsha Russo heading in our direction. I introduced her to Mrs. Lincoln, who ignored her.

"What exactly happened?" I asked.

"You can see for yourself," Selma Lincoln said. "A pair of thugs beat the crap out of her."

"Who were they?"

"They were wearing ski masks. Steffi couldn't identify them."

"Were they swim team members?"

"I just told you, she doesn't know who they were."

"Did they say anything?"

"They said for her to keep her mouth shut. If she didn't, next time would be a whole lot worse. This is all your fault. Steffi was right about you."

She turned on her heel and headed back to the ICU.

Jill MacDonough sidled over to me. "Such a special woman," she commented, with the hint of a smile. "And so smitten with you."

Jill always had a smart mouth on her. "When do you think I can talk to Steffi?"

"Too soon to tell. She's pretty gaga. How about I call you when she's more compos?"

"Okay."

"Unless, that is, you wanted to stick around and keep the mother company."

I stared at her.

"I could probably scare up a private room for the two of you."

"Jill," I interrupted.

"Give you a chance to patch things up."

"Jill."

"Yes?"

"Quit it."

She grinned at me. "I'll holler as soon as she's awake."

●　●　●　●　●

"Something's wrong here, Fred," I said to the Freedom High swim coach, Fred Maxwell. "People talk but don't really say anything. There's a schism between team members. And now one of the girls has been assaulted because she spoke with me. Tell me what you know, Fred."

"I've already told you."

I had caught up with him as he was leaving the gym. When he spotted me, he became nervous. His eyes were unfocused, darting every which way. A thin layer of sweat broke out on his forehead.

"What's a play party?"

"A what party?"

"Don't fuck with me, Fred. You're the cheese here. You know each one of these kids. There's something insidious going on. Something that separates the good-looking kids from the less attractive ones. It's caused a serious rift that appears to have infected the entire swim team."

"Look, Buddy, if I knew anything, I swear I'd tell you."

I was having trouble believing him. My gut was screaming there was no way Fred Maxwell wasn't aware that something untoward was going on under his nose. Perhaps he didn't know all of the details, but a cagey veteran like him surely knew that something smelled bad. And if he refused to acknowledge it, it was because he had chosen not to. I didn't like it one bit.

"If you're involved in this, Fred, even if only implicitly, and I find out you've been looking the other way in an effort to escape accountability, I'm going to nail you for it. I don't give a rat's ass how long you've been here."

He glared at me.

"Think it over. One person's already lost his life. A girl has been brutalized. It's your show. It's time you produced answers to just what in the hell is going on here. And real soon, Fred," I emphasized. "Real soon."

Chapter Thirty

Judy Nicholas phoned to inform me the owner had returned. She had spotted him that morning carrying groceries into the house.

Later that night, I parked my Wrangler within sight of the Meeker Street bungalow, tucked between two other cars. Rather than listen to talk radio or randomly selected music, I had the audio version of Elmore Leonard's action-packed Western, *Last Stand at Saber River*, plugged into the car's speaker system.

I also brought two thermos jugs filled with black coffee, a box of Snackwell Devil's Food cookies, and a package of Nips Chocolate Parfait sucking candies. I figured that between the caffeine and the sugar, I'd stay awake and wired.

It was around eleven-thirty when I spotted a young man exit the bungalow, a backpack slung over his shoulder. He opened the garage door and stepped inside. After several minutes, a slate gray BMW M14 sports coupe backed down the driveway, turned left and drove past me, gathering speed as it did. After a while, with my lights switched off, I followed.

The BMW drove aimlessly through the sparse late night traffic, turning onto side streets and sliding into main drags as if in search of something elusive. This went on for some while before the BMW made its way onto Highway 101, heading south toward Los Angeles. I quit following once we crossed the county line.

It was close to two a.m. by the time I got home. I poured myself a Jack Daniel's and collapsed into an armchair in my darkened living room.

My thoughts turned to the young man I had followed. Was he a candidate for closer inspection? He seemed a fish in unlikely waters, which heightened my suspicions. So, what were the facts?

A real estate trust fund represented by a high-class Beverly Hills law firm purchased a heretofore hard to sell bungalow in a low-rent section of Freedom. A young man moves into the bungalow and instead of improving the property, he lets it slide deeper into disrepair. Turns out the young man drives a top-of-the-line BMW sports coupe and seems to be a nocturnal creature. And the house purchase coincides with a sudden outbreak of graffiti vandalization in Freedom.

What's wrong with this picture?

I had made note of the BMW's license plate and was hopeful it might yield the first real clue in the quest to identify the vandal or vandals.

Flush with the promise of discovery I tumbled into bed and slept like a baby.

Chapter Thirty-one

My cell phone began buzzing and when I looked at it, the caller ID was blocked. I answered and the voice on the other end said, "I need to see you, Buddy."

"Kimber?"

"Can you come now?"

"Is something wrong?"

"I'm all fucked up, Buddy. I need to talk."

"I'm on my way."

● ● ● ● ●

She quickly closed the door behind me. "I heard," she said.

"What did you hear?"

"About the girl who was assaulted."

"How?"

"Her mother phoned me."

We wandered into the kitchen. I sat at the table while Kimber poured us freshly made coffee. She sat opposite me. "She wanted to tell me about her daughter and to insinuate my husband had in some way been involved."

"Involved in what?"

"The cause of the beating. Look, Buddy, I told you that

Henry and I had less than a perfect union. I said I suspected he was sexually involved with members of the swim team. Mrs. Lincoln added to my knowledge."

"How?"

"She told me about the play parties."

"What about them?"

"She insisted Steffi had never attended any of them, but admitted she knew about them. One of her teammates who participated had spilled the beans."

"Meaning?"

"They took place. Frequently. And they were organized and supervised by my husband."

"What else did she tell you?"

"As you suspected, there had been a great deal of resentment."

She stood and started to pace. "So, in order to insure privacy, Henry engaged a security detail. He went outside the swim team and recruited a pair of football players."

"To provide security?"

"According to Mrs. Lincoln, yes."

"There's more?"

"The football players were invited to the play parties."

"Thereby despoiling the swim team's exclusivity."

"That's not all they despoiled."

"Go on."

"In the weeks before Henry died, the party dynamic changed. It became rough. The football players considered themselves dominant."

"Meaning?"

"The sex was no longer consensual. According to Steffi's source, the parties had been cordial and even courtly, but once the football guys established their dominance, they took whatever they wanted."

"Rape," I muttered.

"It appears so."

"And your husband?"

"They threatened him. He was a physical coward and they took advantage of it."

"And?"

"I gather things went haywire. The parties spun out of control. And then Henry was killed."

"Did Steffi's source identify the killer or killers?"

"No. She didn't."

"Does she know who these football players are?"

"According to Selma Lincoln, no one is willing to identify them. The swim team kids are terrified of them."

Kimber left the kitchen and moved to the living room, which is where I found her, in her favorite chair, her head in her hands.

"What do I do?" She looked up at me.

"We find them."

"I meant what do *I* do?"

"You've done your duty, Kimber. You sit tight."

"I'm a train wreck here, Buddy."

"Does your shrink know?"

"About the football players?"

"Yes."

"She does."

"What does she say?"

"Almost word for word what you said."

"That you've done your duty."

"That and also I'm not responsible."

"For what Henry did?"

"Yes."

"So?"

"So...what do I do?"

I wanted to ease her suffering by saying something that might help deflate her anxiety. She was clearly rattled and in need of support. I spoke up. "My shrink used to say that sometimes it's best to do nothing and abide the events."

She looked at me. "It's not easy to do nothing. I feel cornered...trapped."

"Change."

"Change what?"

"Things are going to change. And once they do, you'll be free."

"Easy for you to say."

"You're not responsible, Kimber."

"You think?"

"I know."

She stared at me and then stood. "Will you hold me, Buddy?"

She stepped into my arms and we held onto each other for several moments.

Then I extricated myself.

"It would be a mistake," she said, as if by rote.

"It would be."

"I knew you'd say that."

"My bad."

"My bad luck," she said.

"You think?"

"I know," she said.

Chapter Thirty-two

Sheriff Burton Steel, Senior, is something of a local legend. He fancies himself a throwback to the days when tough-minded lawmen ruled the world. His thesis, not mine. His role models include Bat Masterson and Wyatt Earp.

He is a large man, standing six-four and, prior to the onset of his illness, weighing in at two-twenty. His is a chiseled face with an iron jaw, steely blue eyes, and a thick mane of unruly black hair that he proudly boasts contains not a single strand of gray.

He rules the San Remo County Sheriff's Department as if it was his personal fiefdom. He demands loyalty, and anyone who chooses to defy him is quickly removed.

Sound familiar?

He ran his initial campaign on a law-and-order ticket, promising to protect and serve the rights and safety of every citizen. He won handily. He won a second term by an even wider margin and had achieved a third-term victory in an unprecedented landslide. As was said of the immortal Caesar, Burton Steel strode the county '*like a colossus*,' admired and respected everywhere he went. So you can imagine his terror when his body began to break down.

He first noticed things were not right during his third

term re-election campaign. He started to experience a perplexing weakness in his arms and legs. There were times he struggled just to stand. He developed difficulty swallowing. His speech, always so forceful and commanding, failed him at times, leaving him unsteady and weak-voiced. Regina, who made frequent campaign appearances with him, became insistent he visit his doctor.

He slipped away from the trail one afternoon to see his friend, Dr. Lonnie MacDonald, a highly regarded neurologist, who administered a battery of tests.

As MacDonald later admitted, he had chosen specific tests for Amyotrophic Lateral Sclerosis because he already suspected it was the cause of the Sheriff's decline. He withheld the test results until the day after my father won re-election.

I had driven up from Los Angeles to be with him and my stepmother on election night. I was at their home the next morning when Dr. MacDonald visited. He didn't sugar the pill. My father wouldn't have allowed it. The doctor informed us that although the disease was in its early stages, its progress was difficult to predict. The biggest blow was that ALS was incurable.

To his credit, the old man took the news in his stride. He thanked Dr. MacDonald for his frankness. He vowed to fight with all his strength. It wasn't until MacDonald left and he was alone with Regina and me that he allowed the news to sink in.

"It's a fucking death sentence."

Some weeks later, when he had formulated his argument for asking me to return to Freedom so that I might serve as a crutch for him, he summoned me back to the family manse.

"I need you, Buddy," he said.

When I tried to explain that my home was now Los Angeles and I was gainfully and happily employed as a Homicide Detective with the LAPD, he refused to listen.

"I'm not ready to throw in the towel. With you beside me covering my ass I know I can eke out some more quality time. And I can also arrange it so that when I can no longer function, you'll become Sheriff."

"What if that's not what I want?"

"Look at me, Buddy. I'll be lucky if I'm still around a year from now."

"You don't know that, Dad," I said. "Nobody's put a clock on this."

"Listen to me, Buddy. The way I see it, you and me, we've never been close. But you're my only son. If you were here, we could resolve whatever needs resolving and I could die in peace.

"Add to that the fact you could have a far bigger career here than you could ever have down there in L.A. For someone your age, with your talent, the Sheriff's Department could be a stepping stone to statewide recognition and office. This could prove to be a win-win for us both."

Despite the fact I discussed this with my sister, Sandra, and she forcefully called my attention to the self-serving nature of our father's argument, I still fell for it.

I guess the hope we could find common ground appealed to me.

"*I could die in peace.*"

Or maybe it was simply guilt.

But whatever it was, here I am in Freedom. And despite his protestations to the contrary, we still have our issues and he still has the ability to press my buttons, which he does regularly.

As he was doing this very day.

"This thing's gonna end sooner rather than later," he was saying.

We were sitting on his back porch where a brisk breeze carried with it a respite from the heat of the day. He was nursing an icy glass of Johnny Walker blue. Mine was a Beefeater's gin and lemonade.

"I hope you remember our deal," he said.

"What deal?"

"I'm not playing this hand to the end."

I suddenly realized he had staged this little heart-to-heart so as to trump me with the guilt card. He knew damned good and well I was reluctant to assist in his suicide. What he'd have me do was to stand watch over his passing, effectively playing Cerberus, making sure he stayed dead.

This was a whole lot more than I bargained for. Not that he cared. Things always went his way, and as such, even his final moments wouldn't deviate from that protocol.

Nausea flooded over me and I shuddered to think I might become involved in a deal with the devil. A reality I had feared since childhood.

"We never made that deal," I said.

"Bullshit. You're the only one I can count on to do it."

"But I never said I would."

"It'll be easy, Buddy. I already have all the supplies you'll need. We live in a right-to-die state. What's your problem?"

"Because, as usual, you're only seeing what you want to see."

"Meaning?"

"There are laws in place. A medical presence is a necessity. There has to be a certified judgment in hand proving that end-of-life assistance is justified."

"I'm not going through all those examinations and all that goddamned paperwork. Regina doesn't believe in any of this end-of-life crap. She'll be a total pain in the ass and will stop at nothing to prevent me from going through with it."

"But it will still be your call."

"Bullshit. I'll be lying in some fucking hospital bed with every kind of imaginable tube sticking out of me. I'll be totally gaga, stripped of any remaining dignity and my opinion won't count for squat because Regina will bully her way into getting whatever the hell it is she believes God would want.

"Which is why I need you, Buddy. To insure I make my exit on my terms. Without becoming some kind of vegetable or a religious football for Regina to kick around."

He was agitated and I was the source. I knew him for the bully he was. As was always the case, he believed he had the upper hand because he had a history of always getting his way.

"Don't go upsetting me, here, Buddy. A deal is a deal. Don't even think about weaseling out of it."

I felt myself filling with rage.

"Get a grip." He struggled to stand. "More than once you told me you came back here for the father-son dynamic. To do your part in resolving our issues before it's too late. Be sure to keep that in mind as you weigh your part in our mutual future."

He glowered at me. "Now get the fuck out of here so's I can get some rest."

Chapter Thirty-three

Having been provided with his address by Marsha Russo, I pulled up in front of Bobby Siegler's house in West Freedom.

Located in one of the better neighborhoods, the Siegler house sat on what looked to be at least half an acre of land. It was a Colonial, with rows of hedges and a pair of heritage oaks in the front yard.

It was eight-thirty on a Saturday morning and the doorbell was answered by an unshaven middle-aged man still in his pajamas.

He stared at me. "Sheriff?"

"I'm looking for Robert Siegler."

"I'm him."

After a moment, I asked, "Is there perhaps a Robert Siegler, Jr?"

"There is."

"Would he be at home?"

"I think he's still asleep."

"Would you please let him know I'm here to see him."

"Is he in some kind of trouble?"

"Too soon to tell."

A flash of alarm briefly registered on the elder Siegler's face. "Forgive me, Sheriff. Excuse my manners. Would you care to come in?"

"Might be better if I did."

"Please." He stepped aside to admit me. "I've just made fresh coffee. May I offer you some?"

"I'm good, thanks."

He led me into a den that appeared to serve primarily as a TV room. A sofa and several lounge chairs stood facing a giant-screen home entertainment center.

"Please have a seat. I'll go get Bobby."

I wandered around the room, stopping to look at the contents of the wall-sized bookcase that was bolstered by forty or so leatherbound classics ranging from Dostoyevsky to Steinbeck. A separate section was reserved for more contemporary books, novels by the likes of Michael Chabon and Paul Auster; nonfiction by Michael Lewis, David Halberstam, and Malcolm Gladwell.

The Sieglers, Senior and Junior, stepped into the room. Junior was also in his pajamas, rubbing the sleep from his eyes, trying to recall just who I was and where we had met.

"Sheriff Buddy Steel," I said. "Good morning, Bobby. Sorry to wake you up so early."

Bobby Siegler stared at me questioningly.

"I want the names of the two football players," I said.

"Excuse me?"

"The two football players that Coach Hank brought aboard to provide security."

"I don't know what you're talking about." To his father he said, "I don't know what he's talking about."

My gaze wandered from Junior to Senior. "This can go easy for him or it could go hard. He knows what I'm talking about and he has about a minute and a half to give me the information I'm requesting. If he continues to play dumb, I'll sure as hell arrest him and make certain he enters the system which will be a lifetime stain on his record."

Mr. Siegler looked at his son. "Do you have the information the Sheriff is seeking?"

Bobby lowered his head and nodded.

"I'll take that as a yes," the elder Siegler said.

Bobby nodded again.

"Then tell it to the Sheriff. Now."

Tears appeared in the corners of Bobby's eyes. "They'll fuck me over if I do."

"Who will?" I asked.

"Them. They'll beat the crap out of me."

"They won't," I said. "I promise. Tell me their names."

He pleaded with me. "I'm no squealer."

I looked at his father. "I'm going to take him downtown to Sheriff's headquarters. I'll book him and request he be held without bond. You might want to contact a lawyer."

I approached Bobby Siegler and removed the handcuffs from my service belt.

"Are you crazy?" Mr. Siegler said to his son, the intensity of his voice on the rise. "Tell the man what he wants to know. This could mess up your entire life."

Bobby Siegler looked at me. "Ronnie van Cleave and Paulie Henderson."

"Seniors?"

"Yes."

I looked at Mr. Siegler and said, "Good call."

Chapter Thirty-four

I phoned Marsha Russo from my cruiser. "Two seniors. Members of the football team. Ronald Van Cleave and Paul Henderson. I want you to pick them both up and hold them without bail. Separately. Bring along some backup in case they cause trouble. Let me know when you've got them."

"Charge?"

"Murder."

"They killed Hank Carson?"

"Uncertain. Were I a betting man, I'd say no. But they've got information that in all likelihood relates to the killing."

"Do I need to involve the D.A.'s office?"

"Eventually. But not yet."

"Got it. I'll be back to you when it's done."

After the call, I drove around aimlessly for a while. I stopped at a Dunkin' Donuts and picked up coffee and a cruller. I wandered over to Freedom Park and pulled up in the shade of a live oak, in a red zone, within sight of the statue of the former California Governor and later Supreme Court Justice, Earl Warren.

The base of the statue displayed Warren's most notable quote, *It is the spirit and not the form of law that keeps justice alive.*

An axiom I admired.

I sipped and ate and stared sightlessly out the window. I didn't like this murder case. It depressed me. Which had to do with the demeaning play parties Henry Carson had organized.

But without having even spoken with them, I didn't make the football players for the murder, even though their involvement had more than likely changed the game. They understood they could control Hank Carson because his job was at stake. By threatening to blow the whistle on him, they gained the upper hand.

At the outset I'm sure they didn't grasp all that was in store for them, but when they became participants and realized that a play party was, in reality, a sex party, they seized their opportunity.

Steffi Lincoln told her mother that her informant friend claimed things had gotten rough. Consensual sex was no longer *de rigueur*. The football thugs were in charge. Roughhousing had become a factor. Rape was a regular occurrence. Somewhere in that dynamic lay the answer to who murdered Henry Carson.

I'd have to present this case to the District Attorney pretty soon, but the last people I wanted to deal with just now were D.A. Michael Lytell and his whipping boy, Skip Wilder.

I acknowledged to myself that often the trials and tribulations of a big city police force were a whole lot less personal than those of a small town. This case was a striking example of that dictum.

Then there was the issue of my father. I knew I had to involve him in these goings-on, but sitting in front of the deteriorating old man, forcing myself to once again watch him fruitlessly standing up to his mortality, always took the starch out of me.

I finished the cruller, took a last sip of coffee, waved goodbye to Earl Warren, and headed for the station, where the idea of making the lives of a pair of malevolent idiots more miserable than my own was suddenly very appealing.

Chapter Thirty-five

"The BMW is registered to a Gustavo Noel who lives in Beverly Hills," Marsha Russo told me when she picked up my call.

"Gustavo Noel, the movie mogul?"

"Is there another one?"

"Are you currently on your computer?"

"What's it to you?"

"Look him up."

"Gustavo Noel?"

"Yes. I want to know about him and his family."

"One moment, please," she pronounced in her faux official voice.

I waited.

She came back on the line. "You're going to love this, Buddy."

"Tell me."

"Robaire," she said.

"What Robaire?"

"The son."

"Robaire Noel?"

"None other."

"Robaire Noel," I muttered. "Robber Xmas?"

"You know what, Buddy? You're a lot smarter than I give you credit for."

My mind was racing. Our tagger Robaire Noel is the son of Gustavo Noel, the movie industry giant.

"Catarina and Francesca," Marsha added, interrupting my preoccupation.

"I beg your pardon?"

"Two daughters. Catarina and Francesca."

"Sisters of Robaire?"

"Yep."

"Do me a favor."

"Only if you ask nicely."

"See what you can learn about all three of the children. And get me Pere Noel's address. And any other information you think might be relevant."

"My pleasure." She ended the call.

"Gustavo Noel," I exclaimed to myself. "How about them apples?"

Gustavo Noel was the modern-day equivalent of the old-time movie mogul. His story was the stuff of Hollywood legend. Born the son of aristocratic parents in Mexico City, he had been educated both there and later, when his parents moved to Los Angeles, here.

It was while he was studying at The University of Southern California that he fell in with the motion picture crowd. He subsequently took film classes and produced several short movies, which connected him with such USC luminaries as Lucas, Coppola, and Spielberg.

After graduation, young Gustavo joined his father's vast industrial complex but quickly lost interest. When he convinced the old man to finance his dream of becoming a filmmaker, he was off and running.

He proved himself a smart and cunning executive. Capitalizing on his USC connections, his debut feature, *The Lonely Hunter*, cast and staffed with his college chums, won Gustavo an Oscar nomination. His second film, *Galaxy Wars*, grossed in excess of seven hundred million dollars.

His purchase of Nexus Film Studios, a prolific low-budget production company possessing a backlot and a notable film library, coupled with his own bounteous annual output, qualified the fledgling Noel Films International as a mini-major.

With more than enough money to fund his myriad projects, plus an A list address book, Gustavo Noel soon became Hollywood royalty.

The bleating of my cell phone interrupted my musings.

"You'll be pleased to learn that both Catarina and Francesca Noel occupy lofty positions in the hierarchy of Noel Films."

"I'm sensing a *but* in there somewhere."

"Robaire Noel, the prodigal son, is the family black sheep. He flunked out of USC after a single semester. Although he still lives on the family dime, he's estranged from them."

"What else?"

"He fancies himself a great artist."

"Don't tell me. Graffiti?"

"Bingo."

"Where on the family dime does he live?"

"Cell phone tracking narrows the search to two locations. One in Beverly Hills. The other here."

"In Freedom?"

"Yes."

"321 Meeker Street."

"How do you know that?"

"I'm the Sheriff's Chief Deputy. I know everything."

"Yeah, yeah," she said. "Get yourself some new material. Oh, and Messrs Van Cleave and Henderson are cooling their jets in separate cells."

"The football players."

"Them."

"I'm on my way."

"They'll be pleased to know that. One of them has already threatened to rip the bars out of the wall."

"Terrifying."

"Wait until you lay eyes on them."

Chapter Thirty-six

It's not that they were so terrifying, it's that they were so mesmerizingly deformed.

Perhaps at one time Ronald Van Cleave and Paul Henderson looked like regular humans, but now they resembled a pair of overly developed cartoon characters. There wasn't an inch of fat on either of them. Their horribly swollen musculature looked to have been attained not only to administer deadly punishment, but to fend it off as well. High school football for them likely served as the training ground for a future filled with even greater violence.

Van Cleave was the larger of the two, six-three or four, weighing at least two-fifty. His feral, gunmetal gray eyes were constantly on the move, scanning his environment for threats, real or implied. Even behind bars, he projected a kind of animal restlessness that threatened to erupt into violence at any moment.

Henderson was the more circumspect of the two, standing taller than six feet and weighing in at not less than a couple of hundred pounds. His guarded black eyes reflected evil, plus an all-encompassing hatred that labeled him as someone to avoid.

Both were charismatic, however, exuding an unexpected sensuality that was both fascinating and repellent. It's no wonder Henry Carson feared them. He should have exercised better judgment in selecting them.

I chose to interview them separately and when Deputy Al Striar and I entered the small, windowless conference room on the basement level of Freedom Town Hall, Ronald Van Cleave, his hands cuffed in front of him and his feet chained to a bolt in the floor, sat at the interview table glaring at us.

"Who the fuck are you?" he said by way of greeting.

Our introductions served to raise his temperature. "I want a lawyer."

"Soon enough. You're not under arrest and you're not a suspect. I wanted to have a little *tete-a-tete* with you in an effort to confirm a few facts."

"What's tattatat?"

"An expression," I said. "French."

I called out to the guard who was stationed outside the door. "Would you be so kind as to remove Mr. Van Cleave's shackles?"

Van Cleave's eyes registered surprise.

The guard asked, "You want me to unchain him?"

"Please."

"You're sure about this?"

"I am."

"Okay." The guard did as he was asked.

Striar and I sat down opposite Van Cleave. "Can we get you anything?"

Van Cleave looked at us warily and said nothing.

I instructed the guard to bring us a few bottles of cold water. When he did, Van Cleave accepted one. "What do you want from me?"

"I was just getting to that. My apologies for any inconvenience we may have caused you. I hope to get through our business quickly."

"And then I can go?"

"Yes."

He looked first at Al Striar, then again at me. "Okay."

"What can you tell me about these so-called play parties?"

"Nothing."

"Even though you were a participant."

"I never participated in anything."

"You're saying you never attended or took part in any of the play parties that were arranged and supervised by Henry Carson?"

"Who's Henry Carson?"

I sat silently for a while, closely monitored by Ronald Van Cleave's malevolent stare. I leaned across the table and lowered my voice. "May I confide in you?"

Van Cleave continued to stare at me. He said nothing.

I went on. "This is a pretty informal conversation we're having here, Ron. It is Ron, isn't it?"

He nodded.

"I'm sorry to say that I'm not respecting the answers you've been giving me. Should you continue to be evasive and unco-operative, I'm afraid I'll be forced to change course here."

"What's that supposed to mean?"

"It means that if you don't start answering my questions, I'm going to arrest you and charge you with the murder of Henry Carson. Perhaps you remember him now?"

"I never murdered anyone."

"That's District Attorney business. Who, by the way, is a whole lot less pleasant than I. But whatever happens, it's bound to be a stain on your record. We can prove you were a player in a series of parties that ultimately resulted in Henry Carson's death.

"By participating, as you indeed did, in a number of these so-called play party events, and by serving as Mr. Carson's enforcer, you're implicated and you'll be duly charged. My guess? At the very least it would spell the end of your athletic career. Amateur and pro."

He sat mulling for a while. Then he said, "Okay. I played."

"At the play parties?"

"Yes."

"Which means?"

"Me and Paulie, we made it with a few of the girls."

"Swim team members?"

"Yeah."

"Against their wills?"

"No. Not on your life. Paulie and me ain't into rape."

"Okay."

"Some of them other guys, them swimmers, they were into roughhousing. Coach Hank, too."

"Did you assault Steffi Lincoln?"

"You know what," Van Cleave said, "regardless of what you said, I think I'm done talking to you. Either bust me or cut me loose. I know my rights. I want a phone call."

"Okay." I summoned the guard. "Please place the restraints back onto Mr. Van Cleave and return him to his cell."

"What about my call?"

"I'll consider the request."

The guard shackled Van Cleave's ankles and cuffed his hands behind his back. Then he marched him out of the conference room.

"What do you make of that?" Al Striar asked.

"I'll let you know once we've interviewed Paul Henderson."

Chapter Thirty-seven

Paul Henderson was escorted into the conference room. His shackles were removed and he dropped into the chair on which Ron Van Cleave had been sitting.

He was an unpleasant young man, emboldened by his physicality, and mean-spirited. He reminded me of a snake, his reptilian black eyes flashing, coiled and ready to strike at any moment. He glowered at us.

"As I mentioned to Mr. Van Cleave, we've invited you here to participate in an informal discussion regarding your association with Henry Carson and your participation in the play parties he organized. You're not under arrest and you're not a suspect in Mr. Carson's murder."

"But you busted me and dragged me in here just the same."

"We wanted to insure confidentiality."

"Who are you?"

"Deputy Sheriff Steel."

"Well, Deputy Sheriff Steel, I don't much care for your methods. I didn't do jack. I didn't kill anyone. Maybe I fucked a few girls, but I'm eighteen years old and when I last looked, that wasn't a crime. Turn me loose."

"Were the girls you had sex with eighteen also?"

"How would I know?"

"I'd have thought their age would have been your primary concern."

"For what reason?"

"So you'd be clear about the difference between consensual sex and illegal sex with a minor."

He didn't say anything, although a perturbed look did manage to cross his face.

"Have you anything else to say?"

Apparently, he didn't, as he sat silently.

"Then, thank you for your cooperation, Mr. Henderson," I said. "Upon your return to your cell, you will officially be placed under arrest and your rights read to you. Just FYI, you'll be charged with unlawful sex with a minor and suspicion of murder. Congratulations. You just turned an informal little chat into a capital offense charge. I guess Coach Maxwell was wrong."

He looked at me questioningly.

"He said you were smart."

I nodded to Al Striar. We both stood. "See you at the arraignment."

We stepped out of the room. The guard asked if we wanted Henderson returned to his cell.

"Not yet," I said. "Let him stew in there for a while. Let me know when he starts calling for me."

"You think this bozo is going to call for you?" Striar asked.

"I do."

"Why?"

"Because once he processes what just went down, he'll realize his options are limited."

● ● ● ● ●

It took about fifteen minutes before the guard stuck his head into my office. "You sure called that one right, Buddy."

I smiled. "I want to detain him for a while longer before I talk with him again. Are you able to turn up the heat in there?"

"You mean with the thermostat?"

"Yes."

"Sure."

"Do it. Turn it to high. Let me know when he breaks a sweat."

"Cool," the guard said and left.

Marsha Russo knocked as she entered the office. "You bleated?"

She sat down across from me.

"I want to know the ages of all the women's swim team members."

"I have them on my computer. What do you want them for?"

"This Henderson idiot may have just incriminated himself."

"How so?"

"He bragged about having had sex at Henry Carson's play parties."

Together we walked to her cubicle where she fired up her desktop. After several moments of clicking and scrolling, she called out, "Got it. Two are seniors, seven are juniors, and three are sophomores."

"Ages?"

"Two are eighteen, six are seventeen, and the three youngest are sixteen."

"Can you print out a list of which is which?"

She opened a different window and pressed the print button. The device on her counter whirred into life. She handed me the printouts. "How do you plan to identify which of the girls had sex with him?"

"Tomfoolery."

Chapter Thirty-eight

I opened the door to Ron Van Cleave's cell and stepped inside. "I need you to verify Paul Henderson's statement and then you're free to go."

"What statement?"

"He told us the names of three of the swim team girls he made out with at the play parties. He said you could confirm them."

"Why would he say that?"

"Because he was very cooperative and, as a result, he's already been released from custody. In fact, he's waiting downstairs for you to join him."

"You mean he's free?"

"I do."

"What are the names he gave you?"

I told him.

He thought for several moments, then said, "Yeah. We both did it with those girls."

"Thank you, Ron," I said. "Deputy Sheriff Striar will be along shortly with the release papers for you to sign. I appreciate your help."

I shook his hand and left.

● ● ● ● ●

"The Katzenjammer Kids."

"Excuse me?" Marsha said.

We were sitting in my office taking a breather. "An old-time comic strip that used to appear in the funny papers. About these two nutty teenaged boys who were constantly getting themselves into trouble. I discovered them at Comic-Con. They made me laugh."

"You sure are full of surprises, Buddy. I would never have figured you for a Comic-Con guy."

"Ask my old man. I have a huge comic book collection that he keeps for me at his house. Lately he's taken to reading them himself. They make him laugh, too."

"The Katzenjammer Kids?"

"Yeah. I'm glad something makes him laugh these days."

"Tough sledding?"

I nodded.

"I'm sorry," Marsha said.

"Henderson and Van Cleave reminded me of them. Only dumber. And way more sinister. They gave up the names of the three sixteen-year-olds. I want to interview each of them."

"So you're planning to seek indictments for Henderson and Van Cleave?"

"And everyone else who broke the law."

"Do you have enough to warrant these indictments?"

"Not yet. But I will."

"And the killer?"

"I'm getting warmer."

"Try not to burn yourself," she snickered.

●●●●●

I was alone when I stepped into the conference room Paul Henderson had been moved to after the temperature in the first room topped out at ninety-four. He looked up at me.

His clothing was drenched and his dark, wavy hair was flattened and stuck to his head.

"Fuck you, dickwad," Henderson said. "You and your steam room tactics. I want a lawyer."

"Steam room tactics? Whatever are you talking about?"

"You know what I'm talking about. I'm fucking drenched. Look at me. I want a lawyer."

"As soon as we officially arrest you."

"This is all a big turd ball."

"What is?"

"You busting me like this. Sweating me. You got no right."

"Thank you so much for sharing your interpretation of the law."

"Up yours. Truth is everybody at them parties did it with everyone else and they all loved it. Them girls, they couldn't get enough."

A sardonic smile appeared in the corners of his mouth. "Maybe you busted me so you could get a shot at them girls yourself."

Unshackled, Henderson stood. "You know, there ain't nothing on the planet sweeter than young pussy. Now that you know how available them swim team girls are, how juicy they are, I'll bet you can't get to them fast enough."

I stood and took a step in his direction. Maybe it was the grin. Maybe it was his foul language. Maybe it was that he was soaking wet. But whatever it was, it succeeded in raising my blood pressure. "Permit me a word of advice, will you, Paulie?"

He stopped grinning and stared at me.

"I always say forewarned is forearmed."

"What in the hell are you talking about?" His question was saturated with annoyance.

"You know what scares the bejesus out of jailed sex-offenders?"

He glared at me and said nothing.

"Just for your information, the inmates of the California state penitentiaries don't much cotton to sexual deviants. Never have. Never will. They're not so highly regarded in prison societal circles.

"So, in your best interest, when it comes time for your sentencing, you might want to have a word with your lawyer about the benefits of solitary confinement. See if maybe he or she can arrange it for you. It might just save your ass. Literally... if you get my drift."

He glared at me with venom in his eyes.

I flashed him a venomous look of my own. "This isn't going to end well for you, Paulie. I'm going to make certain of it."

Chapter Thirty-nine

"We may have something," I said when Chuck Voight picked up my call.

"Such as?"

"Does the name Gustavo Noel mean anything to you?"

"The movie guy?"

"Yes."

"What about him?"

"He has a son."

"Are you going to keep playing footsie here, Buddy, or is it your plan to sometime get to the point?"

"Patience is a virtue, Chuckie. I thought I taught you that."

"You taught me how to count backward from five. Four. Three."

"Okay, okay. The aforementioned Mr. Noel has a son called Robaire."

"Yeah."

"Is there any chance you might put two and two together, Chuck?"

"Robaire Noel," he murmured.

Then, after a pause he exploded. "I get it, Buddy. Robber Xmas."

"Give that man a cigar."

"Are you serious?"

"About the cigar?"

"You know, Buddy, this shouldn't be so hard."

"I'm serious."

"So what do we do?"

"We wait."

"For?"

"Robaire's return to L.A."

"You think he's going to come back here?"

"He's seriously tethered."

"To?"

"Papa Big Bucks. I say we keep an eye on his travels. Once he's back, we surveil him until he decides to ply his trade again."

"What do you mean we?"

"We're talking *A Tale of Two Cities* here."

"I'll take it under advisement and get back to you."

"You know something, Charles? After all these years, you're still a grade A ball buster."

"Up from a grade C. Aren't you proud of me?"

Chapter Forty

Janet Swift was the first of the three swim team girls I interviewed. Marsha Russo was with me. We conducted the interview in my office at the Sheriff's station.

At seventeen, she was a fully developed woman, slender and muscular, full-breasted, slim-hipped, a shorn brunette with lively blue eyes, a tiny upturned nose, and a small, pouty mouth.

She had on a sleeveless, scoop-necked white t-shirt worn over gray capri athletic pants. She alternately put on and then kicked off a pair of Tom's dark blue classic slip-ons. She was clearly nervous.

"You understand why we asked to speak with you," I said.

She nodded.

"You know you've been identified as having been a participant in Henry Carson's play parties."

Again she nodded.

"Have you anything to say about that?"

She looked away and cleared her throat. "Am I in some kind of trouble?"

"Not at all. This interview is a routine part of our ongoing investigation into Mr. Carson's murder. You're in no trouble whatsoever. But I am curious as to how you were recruited."

"Recruited?"

"Asked to join."

She started to twirl the small thatch of hair that was threatening to cover the top of her left ear. "Coach Carson, he began paying a lot of attention to me."

"Attention?"

"Yes. He would always come over and talk to me. He wanted to know all about me. Where I lived. What kind of music I liked. Who my friends were. Stuff like that."

"And?"

"He kept telling me how good I was. What a good swimmer I was. How I had so much potential. He seemed to really care about me. No other adult had ever taken any interest in me before."

She sat silently for a while, still twirling and re-twirling her hair. "One afternoon, after practice, he offered to drive me home."

"And you accepted his offer."

"I did. He said he had to stop at his office to pick up something he'd forgotten. So I went with him."

"And what happened?"

"He closed the door behind us and locked it. Then he moved close to me. He told me how beautiful I was. He said he was mesmerized by me."

"Mesmerized?"

"His word."

"And?"

"He touched me."

"Where did he touch you?"

"At first he caressed my hair. Then he moved his hand down my back and rested it on my behind. He pulled me to him and began kissing my neck. No man had ever done that before. I mean, the guys, some of them would always try. But

Coach Carson knew exactly what he was doing and it started to turn me on."

When I didn't say anything, she continued, this time a little more self-assured. "He raised my shirt. I was wearing a tee, pretty much like the one I have on now. He reached behind me, unhooked my bra and slipped it off. Then he started touching my breasts and kissing my, you know, my nipples. Then he touched me down there.

"He asked if I was a virgin and I told him yes. He thought about that for a while, then told me how much he wanted me but he didn't want me to lose my virginity on a desk in some crummy office.

"So he unzipped his pants and he took out his thing. He placed my hand on it. Then he told me to get on my knees and put it in my mouth. After he finished, he zipped back up and, as if nothing had happened, he drove me home."

"Then what?"

"A couple of days later he asked me again if he could drive me home. I said I really didn't need a ride, but he insisted. This time we stopped at the Sleep Easy highway motel. He parked in the back and took me to a room where we did it."

"You had intercourse?"

"Yes."

"And how did you feel about it?"

"Weird, I suppose. I had always thought I'd do it for the first time with a guy I was in love with. But Coach Carson, he was real knowledgeable. Very gentle. I really wanted to do it. And when we did, he made sure I was enjoying it. Even when it hurt."

"Did it occur to you that what he was doing was against the law?"

"No. You see, I really liked it. It felt good. He took his time and he taught me everything. He wore a rubber so I wouldn't get, you know, pregnant. I thought it wasn't such a bad way to learn about sex."

"And you never told anyone."

"Why would I? You have to understand how exciting it was for me. I loved him. I thought he loved me. It was only later I came to hate him."

"Because?"

"The parties. Everyone was doing it with everyone else. Even with boys they didn't like. The football guys were the worst. They'd pick a girl and then both of them would do it to her. Whether she wanted them to or not."

"Were you one of them?"

"Yes."

"Why didn't you tell anyone about it?"

"I got scared. Paulie told me I was sworn to secrecy and that I'd be taken care of if I ever told."

"Taken care of?"

"His term for hurting me."

"And Coach Carson?"

"He turned out to be a different person from the guy I thought I loved. Yeah, he did it with me. But he also did it with everyone. Sometimes two or three at a time. It turned into a nightmare."

"Do you know who killed him?"

"No. But I wish it was me. I wish I had killed him."

"Somebody did."

"Thank God," she said.

● ● ● ● ●

The other two seventeen-year-olds, Jessie O'Hara and Marjorie Battles, had similar stories. Whatever mystique he possessed, it enabled Henry Carson to exercise a Svengali-like influence over any number of young women, all of whom willingly succumbed to his sexual advances.

"It's time," I said to Marsha Russo.

"Let me guess," she said. "The D.A.?"

"Bingo."

"Proof?"

"In the numbers. It's time to escalate this thing. Make a few arrests and see where they lead."

"Indictments?"

"I don't know, Marsha. Yes, laws were broken, but apart from the deceased, the lawbreakers were high school kids. Kids who had been unduly influenced by a sexual megalomaniac who opened a forbidden door and personally ushered them through it."

"A predator who somebody murdered."

"I still can't figure it out. With luck somewhere, someplace, I'll stumble upon a clue."

"A clue would be good," Marsha said.

"It would, wouldn't it?"

Chapter Forty-one

"The post office," Johnny Kennerly said.

"What about it?"

"Wall to wall."

"Perhaps you could be a tad less obtuse."

"Dragons, gargoyles, and a four-foot-high signature."

"Robber Xmas?"

"The scourge returns."

We had just finished the four o'clock change-of-shift meeting and we had lingered behind in the squad room.

"This one's a bitch, Buddy. I say we ratchet up the surveillance."

"When do you want to start?"

"Tonight," Johnny answered.

"Both of us?"

"We can keep each the other awake."

"Excellent idea."

● ● ● ● ●

My Wrangler was parked a couple of doors down from the Noel bungalow. We had stopped at McDonald's and were engaged in unwrapping our respective Big Mac cheeseburgers and at the same time, dipping into a large bag of sweet potato fries. Johnny's takeout coffee was planted in one of the Wrangler's two cup holders, alongside my large vanilla shake.

"That should help keep you in shape for the big event." He pointed to the shake.

"What big event?"

"One on one, baby. It's all Helena talks about these days."

"She's not really serious about this. She's just pulling my chain, right?"

"What are you smoking, Buddy? She's been in training for weeks."

"Training? Nobody's ever confirmed that this stupid game is even going to take place."

"Think again, big fella. The game is definitely on. She announced it in a widely distributed e-mail. All we're waiting for is the date."

"This is insane."

"Correct."

I looked at the half-eaten cheeseburger and then sheepishly put it back in the bag. I had no idea she was publicizing this event. I glanced down at my slightly burgeoning stomach. I'm doomed, I thought.

Johnny noticed my discomfort and a big fat grin lit up his face. "So what's the date?"

"Quit bothering me. Can't you see I'm eating?"

"I can see you're weaseling."

"Stay out of it."

"Weasel," he said, accusingly.

"What weasel?"

"You heard me."

It was then that the bungalow's front door opened and Robaire Noel stepped outside and looked around. He was carrying a backpack. After several moments, he stepped over to the BMW, opened the driver's side door, tossed in the backpack, then climbed in himself.

"The monster appears," I said.

We heard the BMW's twin turbocharged engines roar into life and watched as the richly appointed coupe inched slowly onto Meeker Street.

After several moments, we followed.

Whatever Robaire Noel had in mind for the evening, it didn't involve graffiti. We followed him onto the 101 Freeway and south to Santa Barbara, where he valet parked in front of The LeGrange Club, a trendy disco, currently the it club for the upscale Santa Barbara crowd.

The hipster doorman greeted Robaire as if he were family, and led him past a gaggle of young wannabes who were waiting on line, angling to get in. Noel elbowed his way through the throng and with the help of the doorman, swooped inside.

We watched for a while. It seemed as if only females were being admitted, young girls displaying a significant amount of skin, all with visions of rich guys shining in their hopeful bedroom eyes.

"Not a good sign," Johnny said.

"Not for us, maybe. But definitely a good one for Monsieur Robaire."

"You think he's in for the night?"

"Likely in more ways than one."

"Home?"

"No place like it."

We hit the Hollywood Freeway heading north.

Chapter Forty-two

"He'll see you now," Nancy Lytell said, referring to her husband, Michael, the San Remo County District Attorney.

"Good mood or bad?"

"Is there a difference?"

Assistant D.A. Skip Wilder joined me as we stepped into Lytell's cavernous office. He was seated at his desk, talking into the microphone of a headset that sat crookedly atop his oversized head.

Michael Lytell was a Freedom fixture, a local boy who made good and who was content to serve a constituency of like-minded locals, most of whom he had known his entire life.

On the whole, although cranky and peevish, he knew his stuff, had a widely respected legal mind, and contributed greatly to the well-being of the county.

He was nearing seventy, a member of the suit-and-tie generation, an apparition of a double-breasted past. What was left of his once-abundant crop he kept neatly trimmed. He was clean-shaven with a prominent nose and even more prominent ears, each bearing raucous tufts of angrily protruding hair shafts. His saving grace was his sparkling brown eyes which, despite his irascible countenance, projected sly humor and genuine warmth.

He stood when I entered, inadvertently yanking off his headset as he did.

"Shit," he said, his attention diverted for the moment.

He picked up the headset and placed it back on his head. "Bob," he said into the mouthpiece. "Are you still there, Bob? Bob?"

He listened for several moments. "Shit," he said again.

He removed the headset and slammed it onto his desk. "Nancy," he shouted.

The intercom suddenly came to life. Nancy's disembodied voice spoke to him. "Use the intercom."

"Screw the intercom," Lytell said. "When Bob calls back, tell him I'm in a meeting. I'll talk to him later."

"Yeah, whatever." Nancy ended the conversation.

Lytell pointed to the two visitor chairs that faced his immense desk. Wilder and I sat.

"How's Burton?" Lytell asked, leaning back in his chair.

"Weakened."

"I'm sorry. Please send him my regards."

"Why don't you call him yourself? Cheer the old buzzard up. Although for the life of me I can't figure out why, he enjoys hearing from you."

"It's my innate charm," Lytell said.

"That's what it is. I knew it was something."

"What is it that brings you and your smart mouth?"

"Two birds with one stone."

He turned to Skip Wilder. "Do you have any idea what he's talking about? I never know what he's talking about."

Wilder shook his head.

"What are you talking about?" Lytell asked.

"The Carson murder and the graffiti scourge."

"You know who the killer is?"

"No."

"Then what is it you want?"

I told him.

"You want to indict the two football players?" Lytell asked. "For what?"

"Unlawful intercourse with minors."

"And for murder?"

"No."

"Talk to Skip. Show him proof and he'll get you the indictments. What's the graffiti thing?"

I told him.

"Let me get this straight," he said. "The tagger you're trailing is the son of Gustavo Noel?"

"Yes."

"And you want him jailed?"

"Yes."

"Without bail?"

"For as long as I can."

"Can you make it stick?"

"I hope so."

"You hope so?"

"Yes."

He turned to Skip Wilder. "He hopes so. Will you please handle this thing, too? I've seen this crappy graffiti and, although I hate to admit it, I think Buddy's right, it's a blight. I'm on board for stopping it any way we can."

Wilder nodded. Lytell stood.

"Find the killer," he said to me. "That's how we'll get ourselves some banner headlines. Short of that, don't bother me."

"It was a pleasure to see you, too, Mike."

"I trust you can find your way out?"

"Not quickly enough to suit me."

"That makes two of us," he said.

Chapter Forty-three

It was just after midnight when Robaire Noel pulled his BMW out of the driveway and headed toward East Freedom, the bohemian section of town, a once-bustling neighborhood that had fallen on hard times, but was currently enjoying a renaissance.

Johnny was driving and he followed at a distance with his lights off as Robaire zigzagged the side streets, finally stopping and parking in the lot behind the Elysium Masonic Temple, at the intersection of Green and Mawby avenues.

Johnny found parking in front of a hydrant on the tiny side street behind the temple.

Robaire was out of the BMW, his backpack in hand. He stood at attention for a while, listening, checking the surroundings, making certain no one was about. Then he approached the temple and dropped his backpack in front of the wall.

The temple walls were comprised of aging, caramel-colored painted brick, several sections of which had faded over time. Robaire walked up and down the length of the wall, then returned to his backpack from which he removed several cans of spray-paint.

Johnny grabbed his iPhone and began filming Robaire's activities. Together we watched as he sprayed huge circles of white paint on the temple wall. He quickly added red, green, and blue, and in short order filled the space with random designs that likely made sense only to him.

Johnny continued shooting as Robaire picked up a can of black paint and sprayed his ornate signature onto the wall.

He had just stepped back to admire his work when I rushed him from behind, wrapped him in a bear hug, swung my right leg into both of his ankles which caused him to lose balance and fall heavily to the ground. Which knocked the wind out of him.

I jumped on top of him and grabbed several plastic restraining ties from my belt. I secured his legs and arms with them. He was still gasping for breath when Johnny and I yanked him to his feet and frog-walked him to the Wrangler.

"What in the fuck do you think you're doing? Do you know who I am?"

I opened the rear door and slammed him inside, purposely smashing his head on the doorframe. I climbed in beside him.

Johnny collected all of Robaire's paraphernalia and tossed it into the Wrangler's storage well. Then he got behind the wheel and we sped off.

The entire apprehension had taken less than two minutes.

We hightailed it to Freedom Police Headquarters where we hustled him into the detention center. Once he was planted in a cell, he looked at us with fear in his eyes.

"Deputy Sheriff Buddy Steel," I said by way of introduction. "San Remo County. My associate is Deputy Sheriff John Kennerly. We're very pleased to make your acquaintance at last. And, oh yeah, you should consider yourself under arrest. We'll formalize it once we open for business in the morning."

Robaire stormed to the cell bars and grabbed hold of a pair of them. "I want a phone call. I'm entitled to a phone call."

"In the morning."

He stood his ground. "You you know who I am? You can't just incarcerate me without allowing me a phone call."

"A regular jailhouse lawyer," I commented to Johnny.

"I'm serious," Robaire said. "You can't do this."

"Are you a citizen of Freedom Township?"

"No."

"Are you familiar with Meeker Street?"

"No."

"This isn't going well, Robaire."

He glowered at me.

I lowered my voice to a near whisper. "May I offer you a piece of advice?"

"What advice?"

"Lying to an officer of the law is a good way of getting yourself deeper into the shit."

"Lawyer."

"You should be grateful."

"For what?"

"The food is better here than the slop they feed you in the County facilities."

"Why am I under arrest?"

"You're kidding, right?"

"I'm not kidding. Why did you arrest me?"

"Because I don't like you."

"That's not a reason."

"Really?"

"I'm serious."

"For your sake, I hope you are, Mr. Noel. Or should I say, Mr. Robber Xmas? That name does ring a bell, doesn't it?"

"I wouldn't know."

I had had my fill of him for one night. "You know what? It's late and you're making me cranky. Why don't you think things over and we'll pick this up when I come back?"

I headed for the door.

"Do you know who I am?" he shouted. "You have no business arresting me like this."

"Tell it to the judge," I snapped and left him standing there, still gripping the cell bars.

Chapter Forty-four

It was the sixteen-year-olds who were now the subject of my investigation.

"I'm almost seventeen," Connie Nabors told us.

She was a tiny girl, no taller than five feet, weighing hardly a hundred pounds, little more than a child. Her surprisingly seductive voice was low-pitched and raspy. She was open and guileless, a sweet-looking youngster, wide-eyed and pretty, but with an air of melancholy about her. A pervasive sadness.

"I tried out as a diver. Even though I'm not really all that good. But Coach Hank seemed to think I had potential, so he put me on the team."

We were in my office—Connie, her mother Louise, Marsha Russo, and me. Connie was very self-contained as she sat straight-backed in one of the armchairs.

Marsha had assumed the role of lead questioner. "Coach Hank was what, a mentor to you?"

"He was more than a mentor."

"Tell me about it," Marsha said.

"He liked me."

"He liked you how?"

"He was kind to me."

"Did he ever make advances toward you?"

Connie looked at her mother, then back to Marsha. "Advances?"

"Did he ever come on to you? You know, did he ever do anything inappropriate?"

"I don't understand."

"Did he make sexual advances to you."

"You mean did we ever have sex?"

"Yes."

In an instant I watched her deflate, her already shaky confidence shattered, leaving her with nothing to hide behind. She turned into the sixteen-year-old child she was, her perfidy exposed, her innocence destroyed.

In her naiveté, she had likely come to regard herself a woman, sexually engaged, an alleged badge of honor for someone so young. But she was in over her head and now she stood revealed, a tender youngster, confused and uncertain.

And ashamed.

Her mother sat quietly, her silence a sign of her complicity. I wondered how much she knew and when she knew it. And why she had chosen not to report it.

Marsha urged the girl to continue.

"We had these, you know, these play parties," Connie said.

"And?"

"Everyone who was at them was doing it."

"Doing it?"

"Having sex."

She stared at her mother for several moments, then turned her back to me and addressed her remarks directly to Marsha. "I can't talk about this."

"Why not?"

She shook her head from side to side. "I had no choice."

"So you participated in sexual activity at these parties?"

"Not at first."

"When?"

Again she made eye contact with her mother. "Those boys. They told me not to say anything. They said they'd come after me."

"Ronny and Paul?" I asked.

"Yes."

"You don't have to be frightened of them, Connie. They're both in jail."

She dabbed at her eyes with a Kleenex and then blew her nose into it. She sat quietly for several moments, gathering her thoughts.

"One day he kept me after practice. Coach Hank. He said he wanted to evaluate my dives. That's what he told me. After about a half an hour or so, when I finished, he followed me into the locker room. Everyone was gone. We were alone.

"He came close to me and told me to take off my bathing suit. He said I had the perfect body for a diver and he wanted to see it."

"And you did as he asked," Marsha said.

Again she started shaking her head. "I was scared."

"But you took off your bathing suit."

"At first he just looked at me. Then he touched me. Everywhere. He made me lie down on one of the benches. Then he lowered his pants and got on top of me. It was awful. It hurt so bad. I asked him to stop but he wouldn't. He said he'd never been so excited in his life."

"And you never told anyone about it? Not even your parents?"

Her mother spoke up for the first time. She was a plain-looking woman, modestly dressed, uncomfortable in the spotlight. "When one of the other girls mentioned to Connie you were talking with her teammates, she asked if I would arrange to have her speak with you, too. That's when she told me."

"And you didn't know until then?"

"Not at all. It never dawned on me that anything like this was going on."

Connie looked at me. "I was ashamed." Her voice was a hoarse whisper. "I couldn't talk about it. Not to anyone. But I'm better now."

"Because?"

"Because the son of a bitch is dead."

"Do you know who killed him?"

She didn't say anything.

"Do you?"

"I only wish it had been me," she said.

"You wish you had killed Coach Hank?"

"I wish it was me who had plunged that knife into his stinking neck. I dream about it. I dream I did it. I only wish I had."

Chapter Forty-five

It was late but I knew any attempt at sleep would prove fruitless. As dog-tired as I was, I still found energy enough to pour myself a stiff gin and tonic, plop down at my desk, and open the murder book.

The meeting with Connie Nabors had unsettled me. My rage at Henry Carson was palpable. I'd come to feel as Connie does. I wish it had been me who did it.

I brushed past the photos of the crime scene, opting instead to study those of the swim team members, a collection of youngsters, all in search of their grown-up identities, still experimenting with the lifestyle choices that would shape their respective destinies.

Not readily apparent was the fact that each of these youngsters was freighted with a dark secret. Many of them were guilt-ridden over decisions that had been made for them by Henry Carson, decisions regarding their sexual awakenings, decisions that would weigh on their psyches for the rest of their lives.

I pored over the myriad photos of Carson that had been collected in the murder book, pictures of him standing on the fringes of a swim team photo, broadly grinning while appearing in the center of a small group of team members, snapshots with various students, pictures of him alone.

What was it about this guy that was so charismatic? Charismatic enough to have persuaded so many of these kids to surrender themselves to him in the misguided belief they meant something to him?

Who was this guy?

In photo after photo, he appeared to be brimming with warmth and love for those pictured with him. His focus was riveted on them, each basking in the cocoon of his undivided attention. He wasn't a handsome man, but there was about him an aura of kindness and warmth that appeared attractive.

In truth, he was a monster who possessed a talent for insinuating himself into the lives of others, and in so doing, earned their confidence and in turn, violated it.

I sat back and downed the last of the gin. I poured myself another.

I returned to the file and once again examined the individual photos of the various team members, focusing this time on the girls.

Janet Swift was seventeen, wearing a deep blue sports bra that clung to her well-developed breasts and revealed her tightened abs. She had on a pair of cut-off blue jeans that didn't quite cover her entire behind.

What was it about Henry Carson that caused this young innocent to willingly surrender her virginity to him? And make herself available not only to him, but also to a gaggle of young boys, no more sophisticated than she.

My gaze fell on a head shot of Paul Henderson, the football player/body guard. He looked younger in the photo than he did in person, but the picture served to accentuate a pair of carefully guarded eyes and his slightly opened mouth revealed crooked teeth. His lopsided smile oozed the kind of all-purpose malevolence that made me angry just looking at him.

Finally I closed the file.

I found myself wishing that Henry Carson was still alive so that instead of the swift and unexpected death he experienced, he would instead live out his life in a prison cell, a daily penance for the hateful crimes he committed when he stole the innocence and probity from a group of youngsters who deserved better.

The effects of the gin barely served to dull my rage. I dropped onto my bed where, fully clothed, I wrestled a fitful sleep, replete with dreams of havoc being wreaked by me upon Henry Carson and the two despicable footballers.

I awakened drenched in sweat, depleted and depressed, frustrated that someone had gotten to Carson before I could, yet grateful they had.

I dreaded what I might have done had I found him alive. And how relieved I was not to have had to face the consequences of my actions.

None of which made sleep any easier.

Mostly I just lay there staring at the ceiling, grateful for the appearance of the first light of day and the chance to rid myself of these hellish dreams.

At least temporarily.

Chapter Forty-six

"What would you do?" I asked my father.

We were sitting on the back porch, he in his favorite chair, me on the swing.

It was late afternoon and the cicadas were in force, loudly chirping, providing a discordant background to a melancholic afternoon.

"Don't think I'm not bothered by this, Buddy," the Sheriff said. "That he got away with it. That no one blew the whistle on him. That these kids lived in such fear of reprisals. Makes no sense."

"The football players may have played a role in keeping it under wraps, but frankly, these guys are a pair of stupids. Terrifying, perhaps, in their size and musculature, but essentially witless."

"You're holding them?"

"Pending charges."

"Which will be?"

"Unlawful sexual intercourse with minors and statutory rape, for openers. Plus anything else that would beg jail time and cause them to register as lifetime sex-offenders."

"Why?"

"Because I want them in the system and out of circulation.

They're a pair of thugs whose future will most certainly include violations of the law. I want these offenses to be part of their profiles. Sex crimes. Criminal assault. Stupidity. All of them serving as warnings to law enforcement that they pose a serious threat."

We sat silently for a while, listening to the insects and enjoying the breeze. He was wearing down. His movements were slow and studied. He had difficulty swallowing. He did his best to hide his discomfort, but I was aware of it. "Stupidity isn't a chargeable offense."

"It isn't?"

"You know damn good and well it isn't."

"Well, in their case, it should be."

He smiled. "You think someone else was involved in all this, don't you?"

"I think it's possible."

"Who?"

"I can't bring myself to say it."

"Fred Maxwell," my father said. "The head coach."

I shrugged, reluctant to officially implicate the coach, although my suspicions of his involvement were through the roof.

"You want to bring him in?"

"Not yet. He's been around for a long time. I'd want proof positive before I went after him. He doesn't deserve to be identified without certainty."

"How do you achieve certainty?"

"I've just started interviewing the sixteen-year-old girls. Very disturbing. More so than the older girls. Thanks to social media, seventeen-year-olds are far more sophisticated for their age than were previous generations. They've only known life in the technological era, where innocence is compromised way too soon.

"The sixteen-year-olds are different. They're still children, struggling to discover who they are. Their vulnerability has yet to be corrupted. I believe this circumstance, this havoc that was wreaked upon them by Henry Carson, has caused immeasurable psychological damage. They aren't mature enough to fully process all they've been through. They're troubled and confused. The break in this case, when it happens, will come from one of them."

"The sixteen-year-old girls."

"Yes."

"And?"

"I'm dancing as fast as I can."

"Meaning?"

"My coply intuition tells me we're on the threshold of solving this case. I just hope it comes sooner rather than later."

"You and me both."

Chapter Forty-seven

Kimber Carson closed the door behind me and leaned against it.

"What?" she said. "Why do you have that look in your eye?"

"What look?"

"Don't demean me, Buddy. Something's wrong. What is it?"

"Can we start this by perhaps saying hello to each other? By acknowledging the rules of civility."

She stared at me. She had on a man's long-sleeved blue dress-shirt over a pair of cotton leotards. As usual, her hair was a jumble. She wore no makeup. She looked tired. Weary, actually. As much a casualty of the mess her late husband had concocted, as was any of his victims.

She had about her an air of remorse. Of guilt.

What if she'd acted on her suspicions and brought them to the attention of the authorities? Would she have prevented not only her husband's death, but her own suffering as well?

What if it was her silence that had spawned the murder? That, with no help in sight, the killer had come to believe the only way out of hell was to eliminate the devil.

"I'm sorry, Buddy. Perhaps you'd like to come inside?"

I stepped around her and together, we wandered into the living room and sat on opposite chairs.

"So, what brings you to my door?" she asked.

"It's worse than I thought."

"Why am I not surprised? How so?"

"In your initial description, you neglected to mention that he would stop at nothing to get what he was after. That when the occasion called for it, he could be a paragon of charm. That he was relentless. And that once he got what he wanted, he no longer wanted it."

She stared at me empty-eyed. Her spirits low, she seemed freighted with regret.

"I neglected to mention it because I felt stupid for having fallen for it."

"It being?"

"His line. It was so intense, so all-consuming, so powerful that not accepting it was out of the question. Either you were in or you weren't. Being '*in*' carried with it the promise of unmitigated pleasure and joy. The idea that he was a phony was unimaginable."

She swept the hair off her forehead and looked away. It was as if she had been informed that the world in which she was living had come to a sudden end which left her dangling in space.

"How many?"

"Girls?"

She nodded.

"Several. Most of them underage. Many now exhibiting signs of psychological trauma."

"Do you blame me, Buddy?"

"Do you blame yourself?"

"I was with him for less than a year. He romanced me with more ardor than I could ever have imagined. You remember the expression, 'swept off her feet'? Well, that was me. I didn't know what hit me. He became my everything. I adored him.

It was when we arrived here in Freedom that he turned his back on me.

"Initially, I thought it was my fault. That I was doing something wrong. For a while I was catatonic. Then my sense of self-preservation took hold. It took time for that to happen, but when it did several months ago, we essentially lived separate lives in the same house. We rarely spoke. He was gone a good deal of the time. I told him I wanted a divorce."

"To which he replied?"

"He never replied."

She stood and absently moved to the sparsely populated bookcase where she picked up one of the books that was lying facedown on a shelf. She looked at it without seeing it. Then she returned it.

She stared at me through distracted eyes. She wandered toward the kitchen. I followed.

She took a plastic water bottle from the fridge and offered it to me. When I declined, she dropped it on the table, then opened the kitchen door and stepped outside.

The yard was postage-stamp size. What had once been verdant, however, was now dry and desolate, the result of either negligence or drought. Or both.

She gazed at me briefly, then looked away. "You must think me awful."

"Why?"

"For keeping his secrets."

We stood silently for a while, then she said, "I didn't kill him. Do you believe me?"

I nodded.

"Why?"

"You mean why do I believe you?"

"Yes."

I considered my response for several moments. My opinions

were subjective and still open to further examination. But she was suffering. And maybe my insights might help clarify things for her. So I took a deep breath and gave it my best shot.

"You were as much his victim as were the others. But your circumstance was different than theirs. You were confronted by a changing reality that shattered all of your assumptions about marriage and relationships. Not an easy thing to endure. Either physically or emotionally.

"We, none of us, can predict how we'll behave when exposed to such unexpected suffering. We're human and we improvise as we go along.

"Could you have done things differently? Might you have had a greater impact had you done so? Maybe. Maybe not. But you did the best you could. Nobody could have predicted his murder. In hindsight, had you known, perhaps you might have behaved differently. But you were in unfamiliar territory and the first order of business was self-preservation.

"Killing him wasn't in the cards for you. He or she who did kill him was in deep emotional and psychological distress. Unlike the killer, you had determined to extricate yourself by leaving him.

"The killer couldn't do such a thing. He or she was cornered. Rooted to the spot. Incapable of going anywhere else. Frightened and helpless. Killing him was the only way out.

"I'd bet anything that killing him was an obsession. Like there was no other option. You don't match that profile, Kimber. I never thought for a minute that you did."

"So who killed him?"

"I don't know."

"Why not?"

"I don't know that either."

Chapter Forty-eight

"We got him," I told Chuck Voight when he answered my call.

"How?"

"He made a fatal mistake."

"I realize that evasion is your middle name, Buddy, but could you please find the point?"

"He never noticed the tail."

"You mean he was tagging with impunity, not knowing he was being surveilled?"

"Something like that, yes."

"And where is he now?"

"Cleaning up after himself."

"Meaning?"

"He's whitewashing walls."

"You mean he's painting over his graffiti?"

"Yes."

"How'd you get him to do that?"

"I'm very persuasive."

"Don't kid around, Buddy. How did you get him to do it?"

"I threatened him."

"How?"

"I told him I'd petition for a lengthy jail term."

"And he bought it?"

"Seems like it."

"Wow. I'm jealous. Can I help?"

"You mean you want to whitewash the walls with him?"

"Must you?"

"Must I what?"

"Be such an asshole."

"I never gave it much thought."

"Time's a wastin'," he chided.

"At some point his old man is going to enter this fray."

"And you want me to help with that?"

"I'm guessing that a full-scale outing of the prodigal son down there in bleeding heart L.A. will become a major embarrassment. There's no business like show business... except when there isn't."

"So you want the crimes of the son to impact the father?"

"I do."

"Because?"

"I want the old man to take this arrest seriously. Pay a price for his son's miscreance. Robaire's incarceration in San Remo County needs to be perceived as a big deal. And when the LAPD also brings charges, it needs to become a whole lot bigger deal."

"To what end?"

"To serve as a message to the so-called street artists that huge fines and meaningful jail time have become the cost of doing business."

"Sounds like a plan."

"You in?"

"Let me talk to the boss."

"What do you think he'll say?"

"Depends on how the political winds are blowing."

"Meaning?"

"It'll be the Mayor's call."

• • ● • •

I stopped by the site of the most ornate of Robaire Noel's wall defacements, the exterior of a warehouse belonging to a small welding company, located on Highway 65, between Willard's Crossing and Freedom.

The size of the space appeared to have inspired Robaire to fill it completely. Curlicue designs, massive blotches of mismatched colors, and the largest of his signatures yet to appear in Freedom had seriously desecrated the warehouse facade.

I stepped out of my Wrangler and approached Officer Jason Kurtzer, a newcomer to the Freedom Police Department, who had been charged with today's care and feeding of prisoner Robaire Noel, aka Robber Xmas, who was currently on his knees in front of his self-proclaimed masterpiece, scrubbing it vigorously.

He was wearing a bright orange jumpsuit with the word Freedom stenciled across the back. His ankles were shackled. When he heard me approach, he wheeled around and glared at me.

Charges had been filed against him, but rather than allowing him to languish in a jail cell, I had tasked him with cleansing his graffiti, removing it from all of the walls in Freedom he had tarnished. He was surrounded by massive amounts of solvents and detergents, including ammonia, powdered bleach, citric acid, and sodium hydroxide—all of them having been charged to his newly opened credit account with the San Remo County penal system.

"How's he doing?" I asked Officer Kurtzer.

"He's not what you would call a happy camper."

I watched for a while. He had already removed much of his despoilment from the warehouse facade. He was agitated and uncomfortable, and in the heat of early afternoon, his forehead was dripping sweat. Despite the fact his head had been shaved upon his admittance into the system, he still managed to exude an aristocratic air. He was a good-looking young man, with intelligent eyes and a wide, full-lipped mouth.

"It looks better already," I commented.

"That's your opinion," he said defiantly.

"Let's you and I have a little chat, okay, Robaire?"

"What about?"

"About getting to know each other."

I signaled to Officer Kurtzer, who helped the young man to his feet, then walked him to the shade of a large heritage oak and sat him down beneath it, his back resting against the tree's massive trunk.

I sat next to him. "You want some water?"

He nodded.

Officer Kurtzer brought us each a bottle. I thanked him.

Robaire drank thirstily. "Why are you making me do this?"

"You mean eradicating your stains?"

"Desecrating my work," he said spitefully.

"Why do you do it?"

"Do what?"

"Insult public property and sensibility."

"I don't have to listen to your crap," he said, attempting to stand but falling sideways instead.

Embarrassed by his clumsiness, he hastily rearranged himself, his back resting once more against the base of the tree.

"Why do you spray paint on property that doesn't belong to you? What do you think gives you that right?"

"Why do you want to know?"

There was an earnestness in his question. As if he was as curious about my rationale as I was about his. I chose to answer his question respectfully.

"Because this whole graffiti thing is a mystery to me. Maybe you can help me to better understand it."

"You're serious."

"I am."

"And you're not going to hurl phrases like 'scourge' and 'blight' at me."

"No."

He thought about that for a while. Then he chose to answer my question equally as respectfully. "There have always been street artists. Since the days people painted on the walls of caves. The form is centuries old."

He glanced sideways at me and when he realized I was actually listening to him, he continued. "Over time, all kinds of things were painted on public edifices. Slogans. Pictures. Political messages. Whatever. Street art has always been part of the cultural discourse. It's only been lately that industry has usurped the form by sanctioning commercial signage.

"Look at L.A., for instance," he went on. "You can't drive down Sunset Boulevard without being accosted by every imaginable kind of billboard. Some even electrified, throwing off enough wattage to unnaturally illuminate the night sky in such a way as to disturb the surrounding neighborhoods.

"This usurpation of public and private space is far worse and way more destructive than any graffiti artist's work. You do see that, right?"

"Frankly, I hadn't thought of it like that."

"So what you're saying is you paid no mind to the street artist's centuries-old right of self-expression. You opted instead to support only the interests of commerce. Of big business. It's okay for giant corporations to erect monstrous billboards, many of them several stories high, and then rent them to any idiot who can afford to pay the freight, with little or no regard for the messages they might post.

"But great artists like Banksy, or Shepard Fairey, or me, even...if we display our art or our messages on public or private surfaces, we become criminals. We get arrested. Forced to remove our work from the spaces on which we created them. And why? Because someone or something owns those spaces. Would we have been forced to whitewash the cave paintings because some rich asshole owned the cave?

"It's you who should be ashamed, not me. I submit that my rights to create and display my art are as valid as those of any commercial venture. More valid, even. Just because I don't pay the exorbitant rates these bloated sign companies charge, doesn't mean I'm not worthy.

"The people's right to exhibit its art shouldn't be the sole domain of big business. Just because we don't buy or rent our canvases, so to speak, doesn't mean they're any less valid."

I watched Robaire's enthusiasm for his argument dissipate and fade. "I knew you wouldn't understand."

"I never said I didn't understand."

"But?"

"The law is the law."

"I knew you'd say that. You'd have to. You're a servant of the very interests I'm talking about. You're their paid stooge. I don't know why I wasted my time talking to you."

Despite his shackles, he somehow managed to stand. He looked at me.

"If it's all right with you, I'll go back to obliterating my work now. Making everything ship-shape so that some big deal manufacturing company can display its commercial horse shit in the exact same place where I had created a work of art."

Chapter Forty-nine

Nothing added up.

It was two o'clock in the morning of yet another sleepless night. I was sitting in my darkened living room, perplexed that I was having so much difficulty connecting the dots.

It was what my father had said that kept creeping into my consciousness. How could Carson have gotten away with it? How is it no one blew the whistle?

Although Carson was smart enough to engage the two football players, in actuality, they were a pair of thugs with an intelligence quotient equal to that of your average plant. They may have been a threat, but it wasn't severe enough to silence everyone.

I had trouble believing Coach Maxwell was in any way involved. He had an exemplary reputation and was a longtime fixture at the school.

Yet someone else had to have known.

Who could it have been?

It was during my interview with Becky Nyman that I stumbled upon the answer.

I was still working my way through the sixteen-year-olds when Becky's mother, Clarice, phoned for an appointment. Following the death of Henry Carson, Becky's mother told me that her daughter had begun to show unusual signs of stress. She was normally an easygoing youngster, warm and friendly, successful in her academics, excited to have made the swim team in her sophomore year.

But after Carson's death, something in her changed. She became less outgoing. Her schoolwork suffered. She stopped hanging out with her friends. She became moody and withdrawn.

At first Mrs. Nyman thought it was a knee-jerk reaction to the coach's death. But when Becky didn't get any better, she became worried. "It was going around that some of the swim team girls had been to see you. She mentioned it to me and when I asked her about it, that's when she broke down and told me."

"Told you what?"

"I think it's best she tell you herself."

We were seated in my office, Becky and her mother, Marsha Russo, and me.

"What's troubling you, Becky?"

"I don't know. It's probably nothing. I just haven't gotten over the murder yet. I can't get it out of my head."

She seemed a hardy girl, although on the occasion of our interview, she appeared sallow and joyless. She was tall for her age, well developed, with strong arms and powerful legs. She was en route to becoming an attractive woman, blond, blue-eyed, and pretty.

"What can't you get out of your mind?" Marsha asked.

Becky shifted in her seat and said nothing.

"Tell them," her mother instructed.

"Coach Carson," Becky said.

"What about him?"

"We didn't get along too well."

"Because?"

"I didn't always go to his parties."

"His play parties?"

"Yes."

"Why not?"

"They made me uncomfortable."

"You said you didn't always go to them. How many did you attend?"

"Actually, only one."

"And?"

She looked down and didn't say anything.

"Let me guess," Marsha said. "You didn't approve of what was taking place."

Becky looked up. "Yes."

"How long did you stay at the party?"

"Let's just say that I left only a few minutes after I got there."

"And what did Coach Carson have to say about that?"

"He badgered me."

"Meaning?"

"Every time there was a party, he insisted I show up."

"And you continued to refuse."

"I did."

"Tell him," her mother said.

She looked at her mother, then at me. "I went to see Miss Peterson."

"The Principal?"

"Yes."

"And what did she say?"

"When I told her what I had seen, she got angry with me. She said I was lying. That no such thing could ever happen at Freedom High. She told me that if I said one word about it to anyone else, there would be serious repercussions. She said there'd be a price to pay."

"Miss Peterson told you that?"

"Yes."

"When did this happen?"

"A few weeks before he was murdered."

"What did you do?"

"I didn't say anything."

"And you stayed on the swim team."

"Actually, I tried to quit."

"And?"

"He wouldn't let me."

"Coach Carson?"

"Yes."

"How were things between you?"

"Not good. He kept telling me to keep my mouth shut. That he was watching me. He told me to remember what Miss Peterson had said."

"And that was it?"

"After he died, the football boys...they came around nearly every day. They'd hunt me down in the hall and start poking at me. They told me I was on their radar. They said I better keep my mouth shut. They scared me."

"So you said nothing about it. Not even to your mother."

"I was afraid to."

"And you changed your mind because?"

"When one of the other girls said she had told you what was going on, and that the two football jerks were now in jail, I knew it was time."

"To talk about it."

"Yes."

"To me?"

"And to my mom."

"It's very courageous of you, Becky."

She looked at me. "I hated him. I really hated him. I wanted him dead. I only wish it was me who killed him."

Chapter Fifty

My father was having a good day and had managed to bring himself to his office where, having heard of his presence in the building, staff members and various officials stopped by in droves. Although exhausting, the infusion of energy was infectious and it cheered him considerably.

He carved out time enough for Marsha, Johnny, and me to confer about the Henry Carson murder case.

He looked at me. "How do you plan to proceed?"

"As you would."

"Tell me."

I sat silently for several minutes. I wanted my thinking to be precise. I wanted him to approve of my plan. "I'll seek confirmation from Julia Peterson of what I believe happened."

"Which is?"

"As was the case with almost all of the women he came in contact with, I believe Ms. Julia fell under Henry Carson's thrall."

"Meaning?"

"He ratcheted up the charm and she succumbed to it."

"You mean they were having an affair?"

"I mean she, like most all of the others, was mesmerized by him. Whatever it was he did, however he did it, it always seemed to work. His widow told me she had never been romanced in the manner she had been by him. So much so that she jumped into a marriage which, ironically, might have taken place at the exact same time he was on the make for Julia Peterson."

"How could that be?"

"He was working in New Jersey and appeared to be settling into a career track that would keep him there. He met Kimber and they married. But no sooner had they done that, than he learned about and interviewed for the Freedom High School job."

"Interviewed with Julia Peterson?" Marsha asked.

I nodded. "Turns out he really wanted the job. The idea of living in Southern California was a whole lot more appealing to him than living in Maplewood, New Jersey."

"So you're suggesting he put the bum's rush on Julia," my father asked.

"He made three trips to California. Alone. It's anyone's guess what happened. But Julia was a single woman and she was the Decider in Charge of hiring the Vice Principal. Who do you think got the job? And why do you think he got it?"

"You believe Julia was in collusion with him?"

"I'd guess she was an unwilling participant who, by the time she realized his con, was too far gone to do anything about it."

"Meaning?"

"Were anyone to find out she had in any way condoned Carson's conduct with the students, her career and her life would be ruined."

"Did she condone what he was doing?"

"According to sixteen-year-old Becky Nyman, she did. And I'll bet some of the other kids knew about her connection to Carson, too."

"So what comes next?" the Sheriff queried.

"That's what we want you to tell us."

He was silent for several moments. Then he said, "First I'd verify."

"And then?"

"If things are as you suspect, I'd hang her ass out to dry."

Chapter Fifty-one

Once again the cell phone was the culprit. Hopeful as I might have been, there was no way it was going to stop its incessant ringing until I answered it. I sat up in bed and took the call.

"You might want to see what's about to go on here," Marsha Russo announced.

"What?"

"I've just been advised that a legal team representing Robaire Noel is at the Sergeant's desk seeking to post bond for his immediate release."

"I'm on my way."

● ● ● ● ●

Noel's silver BMW had been towed to the Freedom Police Station lot and I parked next to it.

Three well-dressed persons, two men and a woman, were engaged in a heated discussion with Desk Sergeant Mike Marcus when I entered the station.

The conversation came to an abrupt halt when Sergeant Marcus spotted me. He pointed the three persons in my direction. He stood, glared at them for a moment, then quickly stepped away from the desk and disappeared.

The trio focused its collective attention on me. It was one of the men who spoke first. "Are you in charge here?"

"In a manner of speaking."

The man looked more closely at me and went on. "We're from the law firm of Munro, Furst and Levin, located in Beverly Hills. My name is Harold Green. My associates are William Herz and Janet Robinson."

I looked at each of them.

"And you are?" Green asked.

"I am," I replied.

After several moments, he tried again. "Who exactly are you?"

"Deputy Sheriff Buddy Steel."

"Is there somewhere we might talk, Mr. Steel?"

"Seems to me we're already talking."

Green stood silently for a moment, then looked at his two associates. All three had on black suits and white shirts. The two men wore red ties. Ms. Robinson was open necked. Green appeared to be the eldest, thirty-five perhaps. The other two were younger. They looked like applicants for greeter jobs at a mortuary, each displaying carefully cultivated looks of grave concern as they peered at me.

"I was hoping for a bit of privacy," Green said.

I motioned them to a corner of the waiting area. "Is this private enough for you?"

The three of them made furtive eye contact with each other.

"How might I help you?" I asked.

Mr. Green continued. "You're holding Robaire Noel."

"Robaire Noel," I said. "Robaire Noel. Hmm. I believe we may have someone by that name in custody. What about it?"

"We're here to secure his release."

"I'm so sorry to be the bearer of bad news, but you've come to the wrong place."

"Excuse me?"

"Mr. Noel is being held without bail as per the precepts of local law."

Green looked briefly at his associates.

"Surely there's some provision for a security bond. Mr. Noel is an upstanding citizen. His family are valued members of Beverly Hills society. His crimes, if you can even call them crimes, are at best misdemeanors."

"Mr. Noel is a seriously misguided young man. He's a chronic vandal who has caused thousands of dollars' worth of damage to both public and private property. He's arrogantly unrepentant and a flight risk. If it's his release you're seeking, you'll need to bring your argument to the District Attorney. Now, if there's nothing else, I have other business that requires my attention."

I looked at each of them and then stepped away.

"This is bullshit," Janet Robinson said to my back.

I turned around. "Excuse me?"

"This is bullshit and you know it. Robaire Noel is a noted street artist whose work is on display in any number of American cities. Holding him prisoner is a violation of his First Amendment rights."

I met Ms. Robinson's outraged stare with one of my own. "You're as misguided as your client. This *noted street artist* is a serial defacer. His so-called *work* is a blight on property he doesn't own but sees fit nonetheless to vandalize.

"His thesis as to why he should be celebrated rather than incarcerated is certainly amusing, but the law here in Freedom is very specific regarding the penalties for Mr. Noel's crimes. And they're purposely harsh."

"He should never have been arrested," Janet Robinson argued. "A settlement should have been negotiated."

"Not my table. I'm just a lowly officer of the law, charged

with enforcing it. I'd suggest you take your issues up with the District Attorney. Or the Governor? Or maybe even the President."

She sneered at me.

"Allow me to say what a pleasure it was meeting you all."

I flashed my most insincere smile and left them standing in the hallway.

I overheard Ms. Robinson loudly exclaim, "Asshole."

I turned around to face her. "That would be Sheriff Asshole."

●●●●●

As I entered my office the intercom started buzzing.

"What?" I said to Wilma Hansen, the dispatcher.

"You have a number of messages from A.D.A. Alfred Wilder."

"Thank you."

"Would you like to know exactly what he said or are you comfortable just knowing he called?"

"What are you driving at, Wilma?"

"Nothing. Nothing at all. It's just that his last message was quite amusing."

"Okay. Amuse me."

"I quote," she began. "*Tell that son of a bitch bastard to get back to me immediately or I'll rip out his testicles and feed them to my dog.*"

"You find that amusing?"

"It made *me* laugh."

"You know something, Wilma? You're a seriously disturbed person."

"That's what my husband says," she exclaimed and disconnected the line.

"It's about time," Skip Wilder said when he picked up my call.

"Your dog eats testicles?"

"He's a sucker for Sheriff balls."

"What exactly was it you wanted, Skip?"

"The unholy trinity was here."

"Did you agree to free their client?"

"No."

"And the D.A.?"

"He stonewalled them."

"No settlement?"

"He was pretty adamant. Wants to make Noel an example of what's in store for any taggers who choose to ply their trade here in San Remo County."

"How did they react?"

"Not well. They're threatening to file suit."

"No injunction?"

"They can try. Bunch of high-priced Beverly Hills reprobates. It won't work, though. Not with the way Helena Madison drafted the law. It's pretty iron-clad."

"Good. Was there anything else?"

"Just that I'm looking forward to the game."

"What game?"

"The one on one."

"She told you about it?"

"She can't wait."

"Aw, hell."

"When is it, by the way?"

"Unscheduled."

"Let me know as soon as it's on the books."

"Sure thing, Skip. Probably be when I rid my mind of the image of you feeding my nuts to your dog."

Chapter Fifty-two

"I was expecting you," Julia Peterson said.

We were in her office at Freedom High, sitting across from each other at the conference table. She was wearing a suit similar to the one she had on when I first met her, except this one was a muted brown. Her auburn hair was neatly groomed. She had on very little makeup. She seemed tired and more stressed than she had been at our earlier meeting. Several bottles of water sat chilling in an ice-filled bucket. Drinking glasses had been placed in front of us.

"Expecting me because?"

"I've tried to keep abreast of the investigation. I'm curious to know how you're faring."

"As well as can be expected."

"Which means?"

"For the most part we're dealing with a number of frightened youngsters, unfamiliar with police procedures and intimidated by them."

"Is there a way I can be helpful?"

"I have a few questions if you've got time for me."

She took a sip of water. "Of course."

"How well did you know the deceased?"

"Henry Carson?"

"Yes."

"Not too well. We were colleagues."

"I remember you saying you didn't socialize with him."

"That's correct."

"It was you who hired him, isn't that so?"

"It is. If memory serves, I interviewed him twice."

"After which you hired him."

"Yes."

"You thought highly enough of him during your first interview to invite him back for a second?"

"Actually, that wasn't the case." She shifted in her chair and ran her fingers through her hair a few times. She took another sip of water and began fidgeting with a pen, mindlessly clicking the ballpoint. She seemed uncomfortable. "He was most anxious to get the job. After our initial conversation, he phoned several times and also wrote, suggesting that if I was seriously considering his candidacy, he'd be willing to return for a second interview. He offered to do so on his own dime. He was very aggressive."

"Did he?"

"Did he what?"

"Did he return on his own dime?"

She didn't answer right away. "He was sitting in my waiting room one morning when I arrived for work."

"You hadn't been expecting him?"

"No."

"But you met with him again just the same?"

"I did."

"How did that go?"

"He succeeded in making an impression. He was quite insistent. I told him I had yet to make up my mind. That I was also considering two other candidates."

"How did he react to that?"

"At first he seemed disappointed. Then he began campaigning for the job."

"Campaigning?"

"He insisted we meet later that same day. He invited me to have drinks with him."

"And?"

"I did. Reluctantly. He was very persuasive. He was sensitive to our being seen together here in Freedom, which he felt could be interpreted unfavorably by anyone who might come upon us, so I met him in the lounge of the San Ysidro Ranch in Santa Barbara."

"And it was there that he made the case for his candidacy?"

Our conversation had succeeded in raising her anxiety level. She continued to fiddle with the pen.

"Am I making you nervous?"

"No. No. Not at all. It's just that I hadn't thought of those days in a while and in light of what happened to Henry, they appear to have had an impact on me."

"Would you prefer we stop?"

"No. I'm sorry."

"May we go on?"

"Yes. You asked about him making the case for my hiring him."

I nodded.

"As I said, he was very aggressive. His was a commanding presence. He appeared capable and fit. He was also a charming person, self-effacing and diffident."

"Diffident?"

"Let's just say he made his case by underselling himself. Which was not so with his competitors."

"So he won the job?"

"Not then."

"When?"

"When he came back a third time."

"A third time? You initially said you saw him only twice."

"I'm sorry. I must have been confused. Yes, there was a third time. Also paid for by him."

"Hardly seems like an undersell."

A silence fell upon us. Ms. Peterson continued to exude a palpable uneasiness. As if she knew what might be coming and was terrified by it.

"What happened during his third visit?"

"He convinced me he was the right person for the job."

"How?"

"How did he convince me?"

"Yes."

"His enthusiasm for the job and for moving to California was infectious. Clearly he was capable and qualified. At the end of the day, I felt he was the superior candidate."

"When did you become aware of his behavioral aberrations?"

"I beg your pardon?"

"When did you realize he was a sociopath?"

She gasped. It was as if all of the air had suddenly been punched out of her. She collapsed into herself like a rag doll. "I didn't know."

"You didn't know he seduced half the girls on the swim team?"

She sat frozen on the spot, refusing to look at me.

"When did you find out?" I asked.

She glanced at me and shuddered visibly. She spoke softly, her voice drained of emotion. "I stumbled upon one of his parties."

"A play party?"

"If that's what it was called, yes."

"And you knew about it because?"

"We had a scheduled meeting. When he didn't appear, I went around to the pool house and came upon one of the swim team boys who was in a big hurry to leave. Said he was late. When I asked him what for, he said something about a team event. I watched him leave and then followed him."

"And he led you to a party."

"Yes."

"And?"

"I was devastated."

"Was Henry Carson there?"

She nodded.

"He saw you?"

"He did."

"And?"

"It was as if I didn't exist. He looked right through me."

"You were sleeping with him?"

She looked first at me, then away. "Yes."

"You knew he was married?"

She nodded.

"And now you knew about the parties."

I watched as the realization hit her, as she came to understand that life as she knew it was now over. "I hated him," she murmured as if to herself. "I wish I had killed him myself."

Suddenly she stood. "I can't talk anymore."

She stepped to her desk, picked up her purse and ran from the building.

I took out my cell phone and punched in a number. Marsha Russo picked up the call. "She's on the run."

"Copy that. You still want us to pick her up?"

"I do."

"And detain her?"

"Yes."

"Aiding and abetting?"

"That's the charge. What really concerns me is her psychological well-being."

"Meaning?"

"I want to make certain she doesn't off herself."

"And you think that busting her is the best protection."

"I do. Arrest her and get her settled. And make certain she's under a twenty-four-hour watch. She poses a threat to herself."

"County?"

"Yes."

"There she is. I see her."

"Go easy on her, Marsha. She's damaged goods."

Chapter Fifty-three

"She'll be released pending trial," Burton Steel, Senior, said.

"Not if I can help it," I answered. "She's a threat to herself."

"You think there's a judge around who will buy that argument?"

"I certainly hope so."

"Because?"

"I watched her deflate. Forced to confront whatever flimsy self-justification she had sold herself. When faced with the truth, she folded. She's standing bare-assed naked with no self-invented excuses to shield her from the realization she was duped by a psychopath who not only weaseled his way into her pants, but who also brought shame and disgrace to her sacred career. She's sure to lose her job. Might even face jail time. She's got nothing left. She's the perfect candidate for suicide."

"Have you talked this over with the D.A.?"

"I wanted to talk it over with you first."

"I don't know," the Sheriff said. "You say she knew that Carson was hosting sex parties?"

"Yes."

"And by her silence, condoned them."

"For whatever reason, she not only condoned them, she

also went so far as to threaten one of the swim team girls who was refusing to participate."

"Dumb," the Sheriff said. "Nutty."

"To say the least."

We were sitting on his porch, braving the unseasonable chill of the late afternoon. The Sheriff was wrapped in a cashmere blanket, a gift from my stepmother for his recently celebrated sixty-fifth birthday.

His disease was the elephant in the room. We didn't speak of it, but it hovered over us like the dense cloud cover that precedes a storm.

"What's new with the murder?"

"I have a theory."

"Were you planning to share it?"

"Not yet. So far it's only a product of the disjointed thinking that accompanies chronic sleeplessness."

"I sure had my share of that in this job," the old man said.

"You should have told me about it."

"What, and have you turn me down?"

"I might have, you know."

"That's why I kept my mouth shut."

"Bastard."

"And proud of it. How long before you go public with this disjointed thinking of yours?"

"Not long. I want to make one more foray into the truth before I succumb to the pressure."

"It's the pressure that kills you."

"Another thing you neglected to tell me."

"You take the job, the pressure comes with it. There's no way of preparing for it."

"This conversation gets more depressing by the minute."

"Liar," he said. "You love it, Buddy. You're a natural."

"Speaking of self-delusion."

"Bullshit. The only self-delusion is yours if you don't acknowledge what I'm telling you."

He thought he had me dead-to-rights and was clobbering up to hit his nail on my head. "I couldn't be prouder of the way you're handling yourself," he said.

"Don't go all soft and gooey on me, Burton. It's out of character."

He flashed me a weary smile. "It is, isn't it?"

Chapter Fifty-four

Marsha Russo pulled me aside as soon as I entered the building. "He's sitting in your office."

"Who is?"

"Gustavo Noel."

"Robaire's father?"

"Mr. Hollywood Mogul himself."

"What's he doing in my office?"

"That you'll have to find out for yourself."

"And you let him in because?"

"He promised to introduce me to George Clooney."

"He what?"

"You know what, Buddy? Why don't you just go in there and see what it is he wants?"

"Feel free to let anybody in my office, Marsha. Use it as a waiting room, why don't you?"

"Not a bad idea." She strolled away.

I stepped into my office and was greeted by the movie industry legend himself. "It's about time you got here. I've been waiting for nearly half an hour."

I sat down at my desk and stared at him. "I don't remember you making an appointment."

"Fuck an appointment. It took two hours just to get here."

"I'm sorry you suffered such an inconvenience. I hope you've recovered enough to make the return trip."

It was his turn to stare.

Gustavo Noel was an imperious personage, clearly used to getting his own way, decked out in a snug-fitting, silk Bijan suit, accessorized with a pair of gold cuff links the size of cupcakes. An ostentatious gold chain encircled his neck. On his wrist was an Audemars Piguet chronograph timepiece that must have set him back at least thirty grand.

His abundant black hair was slicked back. He had an over-sized aquiline nose and large puffy lips. He bore the aura of a tough guy, but one with an inalienable charm that was both warm and winning. His attentive brown eyes held the promise of good times, grand fun, and unimpeachable fellowship. He was the vision of a Hollywood mogul of yore.

"I want you to release him," he demanded.

"No," I responded, which was followed by silence.

"Look," he said, "I'm not here to play footsie with you. What will it take to get him out?"

"He broke several laws, the penalties for which are clear. He'll be released when he's paid his debt to society."

"They said you were difficult."

"Yet sincere."

"Sincerity's overrated," Noel said. "The great comedian Fred Allen once commented, "You can take all the sincerity in Hollywood, stick it on the head of a pin and still have room for three caraway seeds and the heart of an agent.""

"We're not in Hollywood anymore, Toto."

"Funny," he said. "Clever."

He moved his chair closer to my desk and lowered his voice. "Listen to me. I'll make it worth your while if you let him go."

"Surely you're not attempting to unduly influence an officer of the law, are you, Mr. Noel?"

"Heaven forbid," he said, flashing his most winning smile. "But surely you know I'm seriously considering Freedom as the site of my next film. A blockbuster, I might add. Clooney. Pitt. Jennifer Lawrence. All of them here for months. They'll put Freedom on the map. The economy will go through the roof. We're talking Hollywood North here."

I had to admit he was an arresting character, clever and entertaining. Despite myself, I was enjoying his company. "Listen to me, Gustavo. May I call you Gustavo?"

"Maybe someday. Let's wait and see how this turns out and afterward, maybe afterward you can call me Gustavo."

"Is this the direction we'll be going in?"

"What direction is that?"

"Why don't we can the crap and see if we can find some common ground, okay?"

"Common ground?"

"You know, a place where we can stand as equals, *mano a mano*."

He considered his response, not immediately ready to step onto uncertain terrain. Then a broad smile brightened his face. "Okay. I like this common ground idea. I might even like you."

"Ditto."

"I'm all ears."

"You and I both know that Robaire has a history of run-ins with the law. He's got some cockamamie idea he's a renowned street artist, which he believes entitles him to vandalize and desecrate any and all property with impunity. He's a public nuisance."

"So?"

"So, he's in jail. And he'll remain in jail."

Noel shifted in his chair, causing his weight and his jewelry to shift along with him. He sighed. "He's been very difficult for me."

It was my turn to lean forward. "The thing is, he's no dope. His ideas are misguided but he seems a decent guy. I can't help but believe he's salvageable."

"How do you know this?"

"We had a talk. After he was apprehended. While he was cleaning up one of the graffiti messes he made. To my surprise, I found him articulate and compelling. Wrongheaded, but not criminal."

"So what do you propose we do about him?"

"You know, if it were me, I'd try to find a way to rehabilitate him."

"You think I haven't done that?"

"I'm sure you have, but it's not likely he'd ever accept anything you would suggest."

"Because?"

"My opinion?"

"I'm still listening, aren't I?"

"He's living in your shadow. Which can't be easy for him. He wants his own celebrity. Apart from yours."

"And that's why he's defacing walls?"

"He doesn't see it that way. I'm guessing he sees it as something separate and apart from you. It's gained him a modicum of notoriety, so he believes it's working for him. He's still a kid and hasn't yet dealt with the downside. As my shrink used to say about me, I believe your son is involved in a conspiracy against himself and he doesn't know it."

"What are you, some kind of Siegfried Freud?"

"Sigmund."

"What?"

"It's Sigmund. Not Siegfried."

"Sigmund. Siegfried. Who gives a shit? What is it you're proposing?"

"How about I show you something?"

"Show me what?"

• • ● • •

We were in my Wrangler and Gustavo was none too pleased.

"Jesus," he said. "My Bentley is parked in your lot and instead of it, you've planted me in this decrepit piece of slow-moving shit?"

"It's nondescript."

"You're, what, expecting maybe a crowd?"

"I don't want us to be noticed."

I made the left turn onto Harrow Street and slowed. Just ahead was Joanna's Boutique, a trendy fashion emporium whose formerly immaculate white walled edifice had been swathed in graffiti.

"Look there," I said as I pulled to the curb, the engine idling.

Gustavo peered out of the passenger side window and spotted his son, dressed in an orange jumpsuit, on his knees energetically cleansing graffiti from the wall. He had been at it for some time and had already removed a goodly portion of his handiwork.

"Well, I'll be damned," Mr. Noel said. "Will wonders never cease?"

"That's what he's been doing for several days now. He starts at dawn and works until dusk. Because it's his so-called *work* he's removing, he goes about it earnestly and quickly. Says it pains him to decimate such outstanding pieces of art so he does it fast."

"I'll be damned."

"You already said that."

He turned to me. "You know, Buddy, somehow, over time, I've managed to make a success of my life. Due in large part to luck, no doubt. But I've always prided myself on my ability to talk to anyone and everyone. From presidents to janitors.

I treat everyone equally and they return the respect. The only person I've never able to reach is that guy over there. My son. Go figure."

"It's never too late."

"For what?"

"Reconsideration."

"Reconsideration of what?"

"Your communication skills."

He looked at me quizzically. "I'm a great communicator."

"Or maybe not."

"What is it you're saying here?"

"It takes two to tango."

"Which means?"

"You know damned good and well what it means."

Chapter Fifty-five

I had made arrangements to have him checked out to my supervision. I showed up early at the site where Robaire Noel was halfway through whitewashing one of his graffiti creations. According to Officer Jason Kurtzer, he was stoically performing the task but was not happy about it.

He looked at me sullenly and was surprised to learn I was there to take him to lunch.

"Why?" he said.

"Yours is not to reason why."

I nodded to Kurtzer who helped Robaire out of his orange jumpsuit and into a pair of jeans and a sweatshirt. He then helped him into my Wrangler.

"Where are you taking me?" There was a measure of alarm in his voice.

"Surprise."

I wanted him to regard me as something other than an oppressor. I hoped we might fare better in a more neutral environment where we could shed our respective roles and find equal footing. It was worth a shot.

We lapsed into silence as I headed for the beach road. It was a typical California day, the low clouds had burned off leaving in their stead blue skies and sunshine. We tracked a trail of wild geese in flight heading north. The traffic was sparse, and in short order, we arrived at Jackson's Crab Shack, a renowned surfer and biker seaside joint that offers freshly caught fare at reasonable prices.

I parked in the lot and sidestepped a plethora of oversized, leather-bound, abundantly bearded riders who had gathered to enjoy the view, the food, and to conduct careful assessments of each other's cycles.

We found a table on the far side of the patio, away from the biker hubbub. We both ordered shrimp platters with sides of coleslaw and fries. I put myself at risk of breaking the law by purchasing two pints of locally brewed craft lager.

"Okay," he said once we settled in. "Why are you doing this?"

Before answering, I leaned back in my chair and gazed at the churning ocean and dark-sand beach. Several surfers were braving the waves, most of them successfully. I turned back to Robaire.

"I learned something when we last spoke. It's been on my mind ever since."

"And that was?"

"Your point of view. I found some form of validity in it. And although I disagree with you, I wanted you to know that I respect your point of view, even though it's unlawful. The vandalism you espouse is a crime here in Freedom. There's no way around that. But that's not what I had in mind when I invited you to lunch."

A harried waitress brought the shrimp platters and beer, placed them in front of us and raced off. We set about peeling and chomping on the chubby shrimp and the greasy fries, all the while swilling our handcrafted brews.

"So you take me seriously. Okay. So what? What good does that do me?"

"That's up to you to decide. Kurtzer says you're almost through with cleaning your various messes."

"My work, you mean. So?"

"When it's done, and you've paid your debt to society, what's next for you?"

"Excuse me?"

"Where do you see yourself, say, in ten years?"

"What?"

"Your life. Where do you imagine you'll be?"

He appeared to be taken aback by the question. As if he'd never considered it before. "I haven't a clue."

"You're what now, twenty?"

"Twenty-two."

"And for all intents and purposes, you're a wastrel with a record."

He took that thought in and seemed weighed down by it. As he fought to come to grips with my statement, I finished my shrimp and dabbed my mouth clean with handi-wipes.

"You're a child of privilege but instead of taking advantage of it, you've elected to squander it. You're not getting any younger, and although you might not be able to see far enough into the future to understand what might be in store for you, I can. And I think you should listen to what I have to say."

"You sound like my father."

"I believe I can arrange for you to be pardoned here and dealt with fairly in Los Angeles. But were I to do that, I'd want something in exchange."

"There's always a catch."

"Rehab."

"What rehab?"

"There's a place we've researched that can provide you a fresh start. Help you clean the slate. Show you that your approach to your art is misguided and teach you the parameters of art world respectability. Assist you in how to re-discover yourself."

"Why would I do that?"

"Because somewhere inside you, you know how bleak a future you have in store for you. That maybe you've misjudged things. And just maybe, innately, you understand that with a second chance, you might still be able to carve out a decent life for yourself."

He didn't say anything.

"Of course, it will take some doing on your part. Psycho-analysis will be a part of your rehab and you'll need to be receptive to it, in order to alter your neurotic patterns."

A glimmer of hope momentarily lit up his face as he considered the possibility of a different pathway. When he looked at me there was a warmth in his gaze that hadn't been there before.

"And you're proposing this because?"

"I don't know, Robaire. Maybe I see some of the younger me in you. You may be misguided, but you're not venal. So I thought it might be worth your while to consider things in a way you hadn't before."

I finished my beer, picked up my plate, which was filled with shrimp shells and uneaten fries, and dropped it into the garbage bin. I motioned for Robaire to do the same.

Once back in the Wrangler, he said, "How would I go about doing this?"

"You might start by discussing it with your father."

"He doesn't much care for me."

"Try him. You never know. Fathers and sons are a singular dynamic. You and I, we have autocratic fathers in common. But now mine isn't well and together we're struggling to overcome our difficult past. And truth be known, although it's no cakewalk, we're both faring better for the effort."

I withdrew for several moments, realizing I hadn't really acknowledged that before. It occurred to me that we *were* doing better, my father and me. Which, ironically, pleased me immeasurably. I smiled. "Who knows, Robaire? Maybe you and your father could entertain some kind of therapy together. Might help open you both to a deeper communication."

He looked at me and shyly smiled. "I don't know what to say."

"Say you'll at least try it."

Chapter Fifty-six

She was lying on the cot in her cell, under a heavy woolen blanket. Her eyes were closed but she was awake. Whatever color she once had was drained now. She looked small and drab as she lay there.

"Hello, Julia," I said.

Julia Peterson's eyes flickered open and she looked in my direction. "Mr. Steel."

"May I have a few moments?"

"Moments are all I have. You're welcome to as many of them as you want."

She stood and stepped slowly to the chair adjacent to the bars of her cell. She sat down heavily.

"How can I help you?"

"I want some more information."

"Regarding?"

"Henry Carson."

She flashed me a crooked grin. "Well, for one thing, he's dead."

A little gallows humor appeared to lift her spirits. But if she knew, she wouldn't much care for where I was headed.

"Was there anything else?" she asked.

"How did you convince them to do it?"

She stared at me. "Do what?"

I had been sitting on a bent-cane chair, but I now stood and started to pace. "I couldn't figure it out. But there was one thing that stuck in my craw. It was the one thing you all said, as if by rote."

She continued to stare at me and remained silent.

"'I wish I had done it.' Which unto itself is an odd pronouncement. Especially coming from three young girls. *I wish I had done it.* Then *you* said the exact same thing."

She stared sightlessly at me, a deer caught in the headlights.

"If I were to get a warrant and search your home, would I find a complete set of steak knives?"

"Do as you like."

"Would I?"

She looked up at me and with resignation, said, "My life is already ruined. You might as well add murder to the charges."

I moved closer to the cell. "Why?"

The last of her reserve dropped away. "The humiliation. The shame."

She gripped the cell bars with both hands. "You have to understand. I lived alone for years and years. My cats were my only company. Men were anathema to me. I had two unsuccessful experiences. One in college, with a man who forcefully stole my virginity. And my pride."

She stared at me. "After college, when I was teaching at a private high school in my hometown of Columbus, Ohio, I met a man and we began a relationship.

"Ultimately, I moved in with him and we set out to create a life together. Then one night, he hit me. More than once. The next day I moved out. I looked at a map and was intrigued by the idea of living in a place called Freedom. So I came here and started over. But I never took up with another man. Twenty years a spinster.

"Then *he* showed up. I noticed during our interview that he stared at me more intensely than he needed to. Every time I looked up, he was staring at me. I didn't think anything of it until the second interview. When he showed up unexpectedly.

"He asked me to dinner and told me he couldn't get me out of his mind. He said I was the most intelligent woman he'd ever met. He fawned over me and made me feel the way I always thought a woman should feel.

"Then he stayed for a second night and after dinner, he brought me to his hotel, and made love to me. I had never been made love to in such a tender and loving manner. When he left the next day, I realized he had cracked my resolve. I needed him. Shamelessly. I thought I loved him.

"He came back a third time and we never left the bed. It was then that I offered him the job, and by so doing, ruined my life."

"When did you decide to kill him?"

"I don't exactly know. Maybe when I accidentally stumbled onto the party. Or when Becky Nyman came to see me. I was riddled with hate. Not just for him. Mostly for myself.

"I arranged a meeting with the three girls, all of whom had been seriously damaged by him. I told them how I wanted to do it. They agreed. We killed him that very day."

"How did you do it?"

I sensed in her an emotional release, the sudden loss of fear and uncertainty. A measure of confidence reflected itself in her gaze. Her perfidy revealed, she seemed strengthened. *The bastard got what he deserved.* She'd face the consequences without remorse, whatever they might be.

A slight grin lit her face. "We knew how much he liked Steffi. So she called him and asked if she could meet with him at his office after swim team practice. She slyly hinted at the possibility of some kind of sexual activity.

"I went home and got the steak knife. He was surprised when I showed up at his office at the same time Steffi was supposed to arrive. He was startled when Steffi came in accompanied by Connie and Becky.

"As we had arranged, I stood behind him and grabbed him in a bear hug. At the same time the three girls approached and with each of their hands on the handle, thrust the knife into his neck and left it there.

"He couldn't remove it because I had him in the bear hug. The girls moved away from him and we all watched as he bled out, got weaker and weaker, pleaded for his life, and then died."

She looked at me, then hurried to the toilet and violently threw up.

After a while, she went to the sink and rinsed out her mouth. Then she looked back at me.

"That's how."

Chapter Fifty-seven

The story hit the media early that afternoon. A press conference had been hastily arranged and District Attorney Michael Lytell, accompanied by Her Honor, Mayor Regina Goodnow, informed the attendant reporters that the Henry Carson murder had been solved.

He identified the high school principal, Julia Peterson, but not the three girls, due to their tender ages.

I was singled out for the part I played in bringing the murderers to justice. I was besieged for interviews by local TV and newspapers, the national media, and the cable outlets. I declined them all, preferring instead to surrender the headlines to Lytell and my stepmother.

Regina greatly relished the spotlight, but out of excitement, she was prone to making errors. She did so that morning, when she referred to the three underage victims as willing participants in Henry Carson's play parties. This earned her a rebuke from the District Attorney.

As my father once commented about Regina, "Often wrong but never uncertain."

I sneaked out a back door in order to avoid the media morass, jumped into my Wrangler, and slipped away. I knew I was headed for the Carson house, but I needed to make certain no one was following me. So I took a leisurely swing around Freedom and in the doing, felt confident I was alone.

I wasn't quite certain why I wanted to see her. Maybe now that she was no longer a suspect, we might approach each other unencumbered. I had purposely not shown any interest in her, but our meetings always contained an emotional subtext that, while unmentioned, was nonetheless there.

She was a desirable woman, and now out from under the shadow of suspicion, approachable. I was keen to see what might develop between us.

The For Sale sign in front of the house offered the first hint she was gone. Once the story broke, she was free to go wherever she chose, and from the looks of it, she couldn't get out of Freedom fast enough. I suppose I wasn't really surprised, but her leaving without so much as a fare-thee-well depressed me.

Clearly, she owed me nothing, but the empty house saddened me. I can't pinpoint why. I'm a cynic by nature, capable of fending off emotional investment in professional circumstances.

But dealing with my father's illness has made me more emotionally naked than usual, and Kimber Carson's sudden disappearance exacerbated that nakedness and contributed to my incipient despair.

I asked myself the same question I had posed to Robaire Noel: "Where do you see yourself in ten years?"

And like Robaire, I hadn't a clue.

Chapter Fifty-eight

The meeting was held in the conference room of the offices of County District Attorney Michael Lytell. They were all there. Steffi Lincoln, Connie Nabors, and Becky Nyman, each accompanied by her parents. Their counsel, the Honorable Murray Kornbluth, also was present.

When everyone was seated, Lytell stood and addressed them. "I'm supposing you all know why you're here."

The girls made eye contact with each other. They glanced briefly at their parents. Then they nodded to D.A. Lytell.

"You will each be placed under arrest and charged with second-degree murder. You will be remanded to Juvenile Court where bail will be determined. Given your ages and the damage inflicted on you by the deceased, Henry Carson, this office is recommending you be released into the custody of your parents while you await trial."

Murray Kornbluth stood and spoke directly to the girls. "Do you understand that murder charges will be pressed against you?"

They all nodded.

"Does anyone have anything to say?"

No one did.

Kornbluth sat and Lytell spoke again. "This is a most unfortunate circumstance. While each of you was no doubt the victim of a heinous crime, you in turn exercised poor judgment in taking the law into your own hands. I want you to know my office has tremendous empathy for what you've been through and we will do everything in our power to see that you have a fair trial and are treated kindly and compassionately. We trust the court to be equally understanding of your circumstance. Is all this clear?"

Everyone nodded their assent.

"In that case, we're done here. My associate, Skip Wilder, will guide you through the proceedings. Please feel free to ask him any questions you might have."

Prior to leaving the room, Lytell motioned me aside. "Are you okay with this?"

"What are their chances?"

"Were I a betting man, I'd say they were good."

"Meaning?"

"This is a high-profile case. A lot will depend on the efficacy of their counsel, but extenuating circumstances should be a factor and I can't really see a jury convicting them."

"Is Kornbluth up to the task?"

"Good question."

"Is he?"

"There are better."

"In L.A.?"

He nodded.

"Who?"

"You mean which lawyers?"

"Yes."

"I'll prepare a short list."

"How will he react?"

"Kornbluth?"

I nodded.

"He's been around the block a few times."

"Meaning?"

"He knows his limitations."

"When can I have the list?"

"Later today."

"I'll talk to the families."

"I never said this, but it's a big-deal case. There'll be more media attention than you could shake a stick at."

He glanced at Murray Kornbluth, making certain he wasn't listening. Then he lowered his voice and said, "There's every chance one of these big-deal law firms would take it on pro bono."

"Even better."

"But remember," Lytell reiterated, "I never told you any of this."

"Any of what?"

Chapter Fifty-nine

I had been summoned to a hearing regarding the request to reduce bail for the two defendants, Ronald Van Cleave and Paul Henderson, to be held in California Supreme Court Justice Terence Hiller's courtroom in San Remo.

Hiller, a buttoned-down jurist in his late fifties, was generally regarded as a no-nonsense magistrate who brooked no fools.

I arrived early and found a seat in the rear of the spectator gallery. As a boy I had visited the courtroom countless times and always stood in awe of its majesty. I admired its rich mahogany gallery and jury box, its stately witness stand, the august judge's bench, and the ornate crystal chandelier from which bounced twinkling speckles of reflected light that winked wistfully at those whose attention it caught. To my boyhood eyes, everything about the courtroom looked imposing and prodigious.

Through the eyes of age, however, its size and majesty came into question. It appeared timeworn now and cramped, its once-vibrant benchmark showpieces grown lackluster; the chandelier dusty and slightly askew; the filtration system barely camouflaging a stale and fusty atmosphere.

Funny how time changes perspective. Nothing seems what

it was. The only constant is inconsistency. I was teetering on the threshold of depression when the courtroom burst into life.

Assistant District Attorney Skip Wilder barged through the swinging doors, lugging an overstuffed briefcase, present on behalf of the prosecution.

He was followed in short order by a pair of court-appointed defense counsellors, along with the parents of the defendants.

I watched as Ronald Van Cleave and Paul Henderson were led into the courtroom by two armed police officers, both boys dressed in dark suits that lent them each an air of undeserved respectability. They had fresh haircuts and were clean-shaven. Contrariwise, however, they brandished leg irons and their wrists were shackled. Once seated at the defense table, each was attended to by his parents.

Van Cleave's father was a tall man, wearing a blue-checked suit and purple tie. His wife wore a black evening gown-like dress that was more formal than the proceedings warranted.

Paul Henderson's father, a senior version of his absurdly musculared son, wore a tight-fitting gray suit. His head was shaved. He flaunted a red ruby earring.

Henderson's mother, small in stature, was in what my mother would have described as a housedress, neatly pressed and clean, but skimpy, too paltry for the occasion.

I noticed Paul Henderson staring at me through dark, virulent eyes. I flashed him my most appealing grin. He scowled.

His father was standing in front of the defense table talking with one of the attorneys. "He's a fucking liar," I heard the elder Henderson exclaim as he pointed in my direction. "My boy didn't do squat to them girls."

"All rise," Judge Hiller's bailiff, Ken Scott, called out.

Judge Hiller entered the courtroom and quickly took his seat at the bench. He glanced briefly at the court stenographer and nodded to Ken Scott, then banged his gavel. "Please be seated."

Skip Wilder approached the bench. "Good morning, Your Honor," he said with a sideways glance at Mr. Henderson who was still on his feet glaring at me. Aware of Wilder's attention, Henderson tore his eyes from me and sat.

"We're here in response to defense counsel's petition to establish a lower bond for the defendants," Wilder said.

The judge stared at the two boys over the top of his horn-rimmed glasses. Then he focused his attention on the lawyers. "Mr. Clarkson," he said to the lead defense counsel, "please begin."

Bob Clarkson, a San Remo local who had defended a number of miscreants on behalf of the County, spread several sheets of paper on the lectern and began to read aloud from them.

My gaze wandered to the families. The Van Cleaves were paying close attention to Bob Clarkson. Henderson Senior, however, leaning back in his chair, was alternately picking at and then biting an errant fingernail. His son, Paul, was slumped in his seat looking bored.

Following Clarkson's statements, his colleague, Royal Morris, stepped to the lectern and began praising his clients as upstanding members of the Freedom High School sports program who had been unfortunately corrupted by Henry Carson.

He extolled the athletic prowess of both boys, pleading with the judge for a reduction of their bail so they could immediately return to the field of play and continue their quest for college athletic scholarships.

Had I not known better, I'd have come away thinking these two meatballs were upstanding members of society, deserving of lesser bail, perhaps even an immediate release from custody, both of them candidates for a bright and shining future.

But I did know better.

When Skip Wilder called me to the podium, I adjusted the

microphone and nodded my greetings to the judge. "I beg to differ with the defense attorney's appraisal, Your Honor. These two defendants are a cruel and heartless pair of merciless thugs. They preyed on any number of young girls and wreaked upon them the kind of emotional and sexual havoc that will haunt them for the rest of their lives.

"As an officer of the law here in San Remo County, I implore Your Honor to not be misled by counsel's florid presentation. There's no way these two sexual predators should be allowed back into society. The record speaks for itself. They threatened and terrified every member of the Freedom High School swim team. And they show every indication that, were they to be released from custody, they'd do it again. They need to remain incarcerated until such time as a jury determines their ultimate fate."

At that point, the elder Henderson bolted to his feet. "How can you listen to this crap, Judge?" he shouted. "Clearly, this guy's not telling the truth. Paulie's a wonderful kid. So is Ronnie. And this so-called officer of the law is nothing but a fucking liar."

Ronald Van Cleave's father jumped up and shouted, "Amen."

Judge Hiller glared at them. To Bailiff Scott, he said, "Please remove these men from the courtroom."

As Scott took hold of his arm, Mr. Henderson lashed out at him. "Don't touch me," he yelled. "Don't you dare touch me."

He placed both of his hands on Scott's chest and shoved him, momentarily knocking him off-balance.

Then he pointed to me. "You're a stinking sack of shit," he exclaimed.

By then Ken Scott had recovered. He drew his S & W semi and leveled it at Henderson. "Hands where I can see them."

Henderson stared first at the gun, then at Scott. He slowly raised his hands.

Scott motioned to the elder Van Cleave and with his pistol still trained on Henderson, escorted both men out of the courtroom.

Judge Hiller, shaken, immersed himself in thought for several moments. Then he studied both defendants. After a while, he slammed down his gavel. "Bail request denied. Court is adjourned."

Hiller gazed briefly at the assembled, then headed for his chambers.

As we were filing out, Skip Wilder joined me. "What did you make of that?"

"The tree isn't far from the apple."

Chapter Sixty

He had asked me to have lunch with him at the house. It was one of his good days and his spirits were high. The housekeeper had prepared sandwiches for us and we had settled in to eat them on the back porch.

The midday temperatures were in the low seventies. Feathery white clouds appeared and were quickly chased away by the insistent Diablo winds. A trio of young squirrels set up some kind of racket as they chased each other up and down the nearby trees. The air smelled of freshly cut wood.

I cracked a couple of Carta Blancas and had downed nearly half of mine before the Sheriff took his first sip. "You're an enigma," the old man said.

"You think?"

"It's what the press thinks."

"The less they know about me, the better."

"The less they know, the more they'll want to know."

I smiled.

"What will happen to her?" the old man asked.

"Julia Peterson?"

"Yes."

"It won't go down easy."

"You think?"

"She led the charge, so to speak. She also aided and abetted. The prosecution will hang her out to dry."

"Murray Kornbluth?"

"Not tough enough. She has to hope some woman's cause will take up her cudgel and provide her with a firebrand who can argue she was as much a victim as the others."

"And?"

"It won't go down easy."

We both picked at our sandwiches. I finished my beer and opened another. I took heart in the fact that the old man was today more like himself. Although I knew hope was ephemeral, it had injected itself into our mutual consciousness.

"People will take greater notice of you now," he said.

"I don't much care about that."

"Your reputation will be enhanced, nonetheless. The town fathers will be more inclined to elevate you when the time comes."

"We'll deal with that when we have to."

"Don't act like an innocent, Buddy. You play your cards right, the greater your chances of achieving statewide consideration."

"Meaning?"

"The Governor isn't going to live forever."

"The Governor? Have you gone daft? You're thinking I might have an interest in becoming Governor?"

"You're a rising star, Buddy. And as I said, an enigma. Once you arouse people's curiosity, the sky's the limit. Especially in California. Home of George Murphy and Ronald Reagan. Media stars who cashed in big-time.

"Based on the attention you're receiving, you stand as much chance of becoming a media phenomenon as any politician in the state. You're a Sheriff. You're legitimate. The proud bearer of the Law and Order standard. Excellent credentials in these troubled times. You mark my words."

"You've gone loco in your *cabeza*. Besides, I have zero interest in politics. I'm just a lowly police officer doing his job. And doing it, lest we forget, in tribute to my father."

"Whatever," the old man said.

We ate in silence for a while.

"I was driven around town the other day," he added. "I didn't see any graffiti."

"It's gone. And the perpetrators with it."

"That's good work, Buddy."

"Helena Madison gets the credit. She put one over on the town council and as a result of her instituting some seriously stiff penalties, the vandals came to realize it was time to get out of Dodge."

"I rest my case," the old man said.

We finished our lunch. The table was cleared and my father fired up a Cuban cigar and puffed it into full flame.

I waved the smoke away. "That's some kind of stinker."

"Live with it."

"It'll ruin your health."

"It's already ruined."

"I'm seeing an awful lot of good days mixed in with the bad."

"They don't mean shit. I'm still a goner."

"I'm thinking you'll be around for a while."

"We'll see."

I watched as his wheels began to grind. I could see what was coming from a mile away and dreaded it.

"We have a deal," he said.

"Don't start."

"I'm serious."

"Why don't we just abide the events, okay?"

"Get your head out of your ass, Buddy. We can abide the events for as long as they're abideable. Once they're not, we have a deal."

I looked at him.

He looked back at me, hard eyed. "Right?"

I stared at him.

"Say it."

"Right," I muttered.

"Say it like you mean it."

I remained silent.

Chapter Sixty-one

I was sitting on one of the benches in front of the pool house, my face turned to the sun, enjoying a momentary respite, thinking about the sudden lifting of the weight of the investigation from my shoulders, but still brooding over the endless recriminations that promised to forever haunt the youngsters who had been debased and abused by Henry Carson.

Fred Maxwell came lumbering out of the gym and was headed for the parking lot when he spotted me. He slowed, then made his way to my bench.

He stared at me questioningly. "What do you want, Buddy?"

"I don't believe you."

"What don't you believe?"

"Everything you said."

"Such as?"

"How long have you been here, Fred?"

"What?"

"How many years? Ten? Twenty? Thirty?"

"Where are you headed with this, Buddy?"

"For argument's sake, why don't we just say twenty? You've been at Freedom High for twenty years. Is that a fair assumption?"

"I'm not liking this, Buddy."

"Who cares what you like or don't like, Fred. In the real world, what you did was despicable."

"What did I do?"

"You looked the other way."

"That's a lie."

"Is it? Twenty years on the job. Twenty years of day-in and day-out supervision of the Physical Education program. Twenty years of overseeing the well-being of every kid who came under your wing."

"So?"

"In all those years was there ever a member of your staff who wined and dined the students? Who insinuated himself into their lives? Who impacted them to the point of sexual involvement?"

Maxwell lowered his eyes.

"Guy like you, who relished his role as mentor and friend to all. Many of whom still regard you as an inspiration. Everybody loves Fred Maxwell. Just like those kids at Penn State loved that child molester. Everybody loved him, too. Until the dam broke, that is."

He looked up and glared at me. "I never touched one of those kids."

"I'm sure you didn't. But you looked the other way, Fred. You allowed what was going on to continue without intervention. You let them all down. Every one of them. You chose to ignore what you knew was a crime. And in the doing, you committed a crime yourself. Why?"

"I wasn't certain."

"Bullshit. All you had to do was open your eyes to see what was going on right in front of you. Every one of these kids was in pain. Scared to death. I can't imagine the number of hints they must have dropped that you chose to ignore. You. Mister I'm-on-Top-of-Everything."

He hung his head and stayed silent.

"I'll wait twenty-four hours for you to turn yourself in."

"What?"

"Twenty-four hours. If you haven't done it by then, I'll bring you down so hard you'll bounce."

"You can't do that."

I stood and faced him. "Twenty-four hours, Fred. It's only out of respect for your good years that I'm not perp-walking you into jail right now."

I turned away but stopped.

"If you think you can skate on this, you're dead wrong. You can hire every attorney in Freedom. You can scream innocent all you like. But there's no way you'll walk. I'm going to haunt you, Fred. Think of me as your personal Javert. Accountability. That's the price tag. And you can bet the ranch you're going to pay it. Shame on you, Fred. Shame on you big-time."

Chapter Sixty-two

It took place in the schoolyard of Freedom Junior High. On Saturday morning at ten. Several wet spots still dotted the court, the residue of a few late-night rain showers.

To my surprise, there was a turnout. A bunch of people whom I would have much preferred to do without were milling about, gabbing and laughing, waiting for the game to begin and with it, the chance to rattle the players with jeers and taunts.

Helena Madison was already there when I arrived. She was surrounded by her family, husband Gregory and their two kids, Vanessa and Greg, Jr., who was giggling and pointing at me.

Among those who had shown up was Big Game James Worthy, the former Laker great, who had played in the pick-up game down at Venice Beach where Helena and I first met.

The deck was heavily stacked in her favor and she knew it. She was all attitude, strutting and jiving and carrying on with the assurance of someone who was expecting to seriously stick it to her opponent.

I was aware of how well-conditioned she was and how out of shape I was. But unbeknownst to anyone, I had been regularly sneaking over to the half court rig that one of my neighbors had set up for his teenaged son. The kid and I had played a bunch of half court one on ones, which had sharpened me and made me somewhat hopeful but not cocky.

I was greatly surprised, however, when I spotted my father and stepmother heading toward the stands, led by Johnny Kennerly, and accompanied by District Attorney Michael Lytell and A.D.A. Skip Wilder.

A number of staffers from the Sheriff's Department had shown up, including Deputies Al Striar, P.J. Lincoln, and the dispatcher, Wilma Hansen. The town librarian, Sarah Kaplow, was there, as were Father Francis Dugan and Rabbi Herbert Weiner.

The presence of all these luminaries served to raise my anxiety level. "What are they doing here?" I wondered. "Are they all nuts?"

James Worthy was to referee the game. He offered me his best wishes, but was clearly unimpressed with my chances. "Just try not to make a total ass of yourself," he snickered.

That same sentiment was echoed by Marsha Russo, who told me she had arranged for a team of paramedics to be on call. "At your age, you never know."

The first one of us to score ten baskets would be the winner, but you had to win by two. I bumped fists with a grinning Helena Madison. As always, she looked amazing and I could feel her enthusiasm heighten when, while giving me the once-over, she noticed the bump of a stomach I had developed.

"Nice conditioning," she said.

"I thought so."

"You know, Buddy, I have to admit I never expected you to show up."

"What, and miss the chance to wipe that shit-eating grin off your face?"

"We'll see who wipes what off of whom, big boy."

Helena won the coin toss, which gave her first possession.

Before I had even adjusted to the fact I was playing in a competitive game, she hit three baskets. She danced around me as if I was a stanchion pole. The crowd was whooping and hollering, most of them jeering me.

Now it was my ball and I took a deep breath. Making use of my weight advantage, I succeeded in backing her into the post, feinting left, and then sliding around her to the right and scoring.

Three to one.

This time when she had the ball, I played defense. I guarded her closely, bumping and shoving and continually slapping at the ball. Which caught her by surprise. So much so that I succeeded in stealing it and scoring again.

She launched an off-balance two-hander that missed, and I, in turn, hit an outside jumper.

Three to three.

We exchanged baskets until we were tied at eight.

Our respective defenses had tightened considerably and we were now playing tough and close. She was throwing her bony elbows at me with impunity and I was constantly hip-checking her.

We were both breathing heavily when I put on an unexpected burst of speed and managed to glide past her for a layup to take the lead.

I heard a giddy Marsha Russo shouting, "Medic," from the sidelines.

Helena managed to elude me and downed a hail Mary from the top of the key to tie. It remained that way until the score was twelve to eleven, her lead.

Talk about pressure. Seeing the look of near total exhaustion on my face, Worthy took his time in turning the ball over to me. "Do your best not to die on this possession," he said.

I whispered my response in his ear.

Helena established her position, extended her outstretched arms, and began waving them in my face. When I feinted as if I were going to move right, she blocked the lane, figuring she would steal the ball and leave me standing flat-footed.

But her mistake came when I took a step backward as if to shoot and she rushed me, her arms wildly slapping at the ball. When she missed, it opened up the lane.

Instinctively sensing my advantage, I rallied whatever was left of my stamina, and raced past her toward the basket. I could feel her gaining on me as we both ran full-steam forward. Then I stutter-stepped and deked to the right. She barreled by me, allowing me to slow down and score an easy jumper from the key.

Twelve twelve.

I nodded to Big Game James.

He held the ball in the air and, as we had agreed, he blew his whistle and yelled, "Game ends in a tie. Twelve Twelve. Both players win."

At first, a stunned silence came over the crowd. Then the applause began, followed by the cheering. Everyone rushed the court, congratulating us both on a game that had been well played beyond their expectations.

I saw Helena's husband, Gregory, smiling and giving me a thumbs-up. My father and stepmother made their way to my side and the two of them uncharacteristically locked me in a three-way bear hug.

Helena and I managed to find each other amid all the back-slapping and hugging.

"Good game, Geezer," she snarled.

"Ditto."

"Rematch?"

"In your dreams."

We were enveloped by our respective friends and family.

Hugs and kisses all around. Their warmth and joy was infectious.

As I gazed at this ragtag group who had come here to be with us, I found myself dumbstruck with unanticipated emotion.

For the moment, I was totally happy, experiencing happiness as a state of being. The cynic in me regarded this as nothing more than a passing change of emphasis.

But cynicism aside, here I was among friends and family. And, like it or not, I was home.

At least for now.

Author's Note

San Remo County, plus its cities, including Freedom, is a fictional place. No such cities in this fictional county exist in the State of California.

Acknowledgments

WITH GRATITUDE...

...to the amazing, multi-talented Poisoned Pen Press gang... Diane DiBiase, Holli Roach, Beth Deveny, and Raj Dayal,
...to the inimitable Michael Barson,
...to the intrepid Annette Rogers,
...to the pluperfect Barbara Peters,
...and to Robert Rosenwald, who makes the trains run on time.

AND TO MY EXTRAORDINARY TEAM...

...Steven Brandman, Miles Brandman, Roy Gnan, and Melanie Mintz,
...with special thanks to Tom Distler,
...and to my longtime friend and partner, Tom Selleck,
...and to Helen Brann and the Parkers, Bob and Joan, whom I miss every single day.

To see more Poisoned Pen Press titles:

Visit our website:
poisonedpenpress.com
Request a digital catalog:
info@poisonedpenpress.com